PERIL AT END HOUSE

Appointment with Death
The Body in the Library
By the Pricking of My Thumbs
A Caribbean Mystery
Cat Among the Pigeons
The Clocks
Curtain: Poirot's Last Case
Dead Man's Folly
Death Comes as the End
Death on the Nile
Dumb Witness
Elephants Can Remember
Endless Night
Evil Under the Sun
Five Little Pigs
4.50 From Paddington
Hallowe'en Party
The Hollow
The Mirror Crack'd from Side to Side
Murder on the Orient Express
Nemesis
One Two Buckle My Shoe
Ordeal by Innocence
Partners in Crime
Passenger to Frankfurt
Poirot's Early Cases
The Postern of Fate
Sad Cypress
Sparkling Cyanide
Sleeping Murder
Three Act Tragedy
The Third Girl
ETC., ETC.

The Greenway Collected Edition
ABC Murders
At Bertram's Hotel
Cards on the Table
Crooked House
Destination Unknown
Death in the Clouds
Hercule Poirot's Christmas
The Labours of Hercules
Lord Edgware Dies
The Moving Finger
Murder at the Vicarage
A Murder is Announced
The Murder of Roger Ackroyd
The Mystery of the Blue Train
N or M
Ten Little Niggers
They Came to Baghdad
They Do It With Mirrors
Towards Zero
Three Act Tragedy
The Thirteen Problems
Why Didn't They Ask Evans?

Biography
Come Tell Me How You Live
Agatha Christie: An Autobiography

Peril at End House

AGATHA CHRISTIE

The Crime Club
Collins, 14 St. James's Place, London

First published 1932
This edition 1980

ISBN 0 00 231675 7
© Agatha Christie 1932

Made and printed in Great Britain by
William Collins Sons & Co. Ltd, Glasgow

To EDEN PHILLPOTTS

To whom I shall always be grateful for his friendship and the encouragement he gave me many years ago

CONTENTS

CHAPTER I

THE MAJESTIC HOTEL

No seaside town in the south of England is, I think, as attractive at St. Loo. It is well named the Queen of Watering Places and reminds one forcibly of the Riviera. The Cornish coast is to my mind every bit as fascinating as that of the south of France.

I remarked as much to my friend, Hercule Poirot.

" So it said on our menu in the restaurant car yesterday, *mon ami*. Your remark is not original."

" But don't you agree ? "

He was smiling to himself and did not at once answer my question. I repeated it.

" A thousand pardons, Hastings. My thoughts were wandering. Wandering indeed to that part of the world you mentioned just now."

" The south of France ? "

" Yes. I was thinking of that last winter that I spent there and of the events which occurred."

I remembered. A murder had been committed on the Blue Train, and the mystery—a complicated and baffling one—had been solved by Poirot with his usual unerring acumen.

" How I wish I had been with you," I said with deep regret.

" I too," said Poirot. " Your experience would have been invaluable to me."

9

I looked at him sideways. As a result of long habit, I distrust his compliments, but he appeared perfectly serious. And after all, why not ? I have a very long experience of the methods he employs.

"What I particularly missed was your vivid imagination, Hastings," he went on dreamily. "One needs a certain amount of light relief. My valet, Georges, an admirable man with whom I sometimes permitted myself to discuss a point, has no imagination whatever."

This remark seemed to me quite irrelevant.

"Tell me, Poirot," I said. "Are you never tempted to renew your activities ? This passive life——"

"Suits me admirably, my friend. To sit in the sun—what could be more charming ? To step from your pedestal at the zenith of your fame—what could be a grander gesture ? They say of me : ' *That is Hercule Poirot !—The great—the unique !—There was never any one like him, there never will be !* ' *Eh bien*—I am satisfied. I ask no more. I am modest."

I should not myself have used the word *modest*. It seemed to me that my little friend's egotism had certainly not declined with his years. He leaned back in his chair, caressing his moustache and almost purring with self-satisfaction.

We were sitting on one of the terraces of the Majestic Hotel. It is the biggest hotel in St. Loo and stands in its own grounds on a headland overlooking the sea. The gardens of the hotel lay below us freely interspersed with palm trees. The sea was of a deep

and lovely blue, the sky clear and the sun shining
with all the single-hearted fervour an August sun
should (but in England so often does not) have.
There was a vigorous humming of bees, a pleasant
sound—and altogether nothing could have been
more ideal.

We had only arrived last night, and this was the
first morning of what we proposed should be a
week's stay. If only these weather conditions continued, we should indeed have a perfect holiday.

I picked up the morning paper which had fallen
from my hand and resumed my perusal of the morning's news. The political situation seemed un-
satisfactory, but uninteresting, there was trouble in
China, there was a long account of a rumoured City
swindle, but on the whole there was no news of a
very thrilling order.

" Curious thing this parrot disease," I remarked,
as I turned the sheet.

" Very curious."

" Two more deaths at Leeds, I see."

" Most regrettable."

I turned a page.

" Still no news of that flying fellow, Seton, in his
round-the-world flight. Pretty plucky, these fellows.
That amphibian machine of his, the *Albatross*, must
be a great invention. Too bad if he's gone west.
Not that they've given up hope yet. He may have
made one of the Pacific islands."

" The Solomon islanders are still cannibals, are
they not ? " inquired Poirot pleasantly.

" Must be a fine fellow. That sort of thing makes

one feel it's a good thing to be an Englishman after all."

" It consoles for the defeats at Wimbledon," said Poirot.

" I—I didn't mean," I began.

My friend waved my attempted apology aside gracefully.

" Me," he announced. " I am not amphibian, like the machine of the poor Captain Seton, but I am cosmopolitan. And for the English I have always had, as you know, a great admiration. The thorough way, for instance, in which they read the daily paper."

My attention had strayed to political news.

" They seem to be giving the Home Secretary a pretty bad time of it," I remarked with a chuckle.

" The poor man. He has his troubles, that one. Ah ! yes. So much so that he seeks for help in the most improbable quarters."

I stared at him.

With a slight smile, Poirot drew from his pocket his morning's correspondence, neatly secured by a rubber band. From this he selected one letter which he tossed across to me.

" It must have missed us yesterday," he said.

I read the letter with a pleasurable feeling of excitement.

" But, Poirot," I cried. " This is most flattering ! "

" You think so, my friend ? "

" He speaks in the warmest terms of your ability."

" He is right," said Poirot, modestly averting his eyes.

" He begs you to investigate this matter for him —puts it as a personal favour."

" Quite so. It is unnecessary to repeat all this to me. You understand, my dear Hastings. I have read the letter myself."

" It's too bad," I cried. " This will put an end to our holiday."

" No, no, *calmez vous*—there is no question of that."

" But the Home Secretary says the matter is urgent."

" He may be right—or again he may not. These politicians they are easily excited I have seen myself, in the Chambre des Deputés in Paris——"

" Yes, yes, but Poirot, surely we ought to be making arrangements ? The express to London has gone—it leaves at twelve o'clock. The next——"

" Calm yourself, Hastings, calm yourself, I pray of you ! Always the excitement, the agitation. We are not going to London to-day—nor yet to-morrow."

" But this summons——"

" Does not concern me. I do not belong to your police force, Hastings. I am asked to undertake a case as a private investigator. I refuse."

" You *refuse* ? "

" Certainly. I write with perfect politeness, tender my regrets, my apologies, explain that I am completely desolated—but what will you ? I have retired—I am finished."

" You are not finished," I exclaimed warmly.

Poirot patted my knee.

" There speaks the good friend—the faithful dog.

And you have reason, too. The grey cells, they still function—the order, the method—it is still there. But when I have retired, my friend, I have retired ! It is finished ! I am not a stage favourite who gives the world a dozen farewells. In all generosity I say : let the young men have a chance. They may possibly do something creditable. I doubt it, but they may. Anyway they will do well enough for this doubtless tiresome affair of the Home Secretary's."

" But, Poirot, the compliment ! "

" Me, I am above compliments. The Home Secretary, being a man of sense, realises that if he can only obtain my services all will be successful. What will you ? He is unlucky. Hercule Poirot has solved his last case."

I looked at him. In my heart of hearts I deplored his obstinacy. The solving of such a case as was indicated might add still further lustre to his already world-wide reputation. Nevertheless I could not but admire his unyielding attitude.

Suddenly a thought struck me and I smiled.

" I wonder," I said, " that you are not afraid. Such an emphatic pronouncement will surely tempt the gods."

" Impossible," he replied, " that anyone should shake the decision of Hercule Poirot."

" *Impossible*, Poirot ? "

" You are right, *mon ami*, one should not use such a word. *Eh, ma foi*, I do not say that if a bullet should strike the wall by my head, I would not investigate the matter ! One is human after all ! "

I smiled. A little pebble had just struck the

terrace beside us, and Poirot's fanciful analogy from it tickled my fancy. He stooped now and picked up the pebble as he went on.

"Yes—one is human. One is the sleeping dog— well and good, but the sleeping dog can be roused. There is a proverb in your language that says so."

"In fact," I said, "if you find a dagger planted by your pillow to-morrow morning—let the criminal who put it there beware!"

He nodded, but rather absently.

Suddenly, to my surprise, he rose and descended the couple of steps that led from the terrace to the garden. As he did so, a girl came into sight hurrying up towards us.

I had just registered the impression that she was a decidedly pretty girl when my attention was drawn to Poirot who, not looking where he was going, had stumbled over a root and fallen heavily. He was just abreast of the girl at the time and she and I between us helped him to his feet. My attention was naturally on my friend, but I was conscious of an impression of dark hair, an impish face and big dark blue eyes.

"A thousand pardons," stammered Poirot. "Mademoiselle, you are most kind. I regret exceedingly—ouch!—my foot he pains me considerably. No, no, it is nothing really—the turned ankle, that is all. In a few minutes all will be well. But if you could help me, Hastings—you and Mademoiselle between you, if she will be so very kind. I am ashamed to ask it of her."

With me on the one side and the girl on the other we soon got Poirot on to a chair on the terrace. I then sug~ested fetching a doctor, but this my friend negatived sharply.

" It is nothing, I tell you. The ankle turned, that is all. Painful for the moment, but soon over." He made a grimace. " See, in a little minute I shall have forgotten. Mademoiselle, I thank you a thousand times. You were most kind. Sit down, I beg of you."

The girl took a chair.

" It's nothing," she said. " But I wish you would let it be seen to."

" Mademoiselle, I assure you, it is a *bagatelle* ! In the pleasure of your society the pain passes already."

The girl laughed.

" That's good."

" What about a cocktail ? " I suggested. " It's just about the time."

" Well——" She hesitated. " Thanks very much."

" Martini ? "

" Yes, please—dry Martini."

I went off. On my return, after having ordered the drinks, I found Poirot and the girl engaged in animated conversation.

" Imagine, Hastings," he said, " that house there —the one on the point—that we have admired so much, it belongs to Mademoiselle here."

" Indeed ? " I said, though I was unable to recall having expressed any admiration. In fact I had hardly noticed the house. " It looks rather eerie and imposing standing there by itself far from anything."

" It's called End House," said the girl. " I love it —but it's a tumble-down old place. Going to rack and ruin."

" You are the last of an old family, Mademoiselle? "

" Oh! we're nothing important. But there have been Buckleys here for two or three hundred years. My brother died three years ago, so I'm the last of the family."

" That is sad. You live there alone, Mademoiselle? "

" Oh! I'm away a good deal and when I'm at home there's usually a cheery crowd coming and going."

" That is so modern. Me, I was picturing you in a dark mysterious mansion, haunted by a family curse."

" How marvellous! What a picturesque imagination you must have. No, it's not haunted. Or if so, the ghost is a beneficent one. I've had three escapes from sudden death in as many days, so I must bear a charmed life."

Poirot sat up alertly.

" Escapes from death? That sounds interesting, Mademoiselle."

" Oh! they weren't very thrilling. Just accidents, you know." She jerked her head sharply as a wasp flew past. " Curse these wasps. There must be a nest of them round here."

" The bees and the wasps—you do not like them, Mademoiselle? You have been stung—yes? "

" No—but I hate the way they come right past your face."

" The bee in the bonnet," said Poirot. " Your English phrase."

At that moment the cocktails arrived. We all

B

held up our glasses and made the usual inane observations.

"I'm due in the hotel for cocktails, really," said Miss Buckley. "I expect they're wondering what has become of me."

Poirot cleared his throat and set down his glass.

"Ah! for a cup of good rich chocolate," he murmured. "But in England they make it not. Still, in England you have some very pleasing customs. The young girls, their hats they come on and off—so prettily—so easily——"

The girl stared at him.

"What do you mean? Why shouldn't they?"

"You ask that because you are young—so young, Mademoiselle. But to me the natural thing seems to have a coiffure high and rigid—so—and the hat attached with many hatpins—*là—là—là—et là*."

He executed four vicious jabs in the air.

"But how frightfully uncomfortable!"

"Ah! I should think so," said Poirot. No martyred lady could have spoken with more feeling. "When the wind blew it was the agony—it gave you the *migraine*."

Miss Buckley dragged off the simple wide-brimmed felt she was wearing and cast it down beside her.

"And now we do this," she laughed.

"Which is sensible and charming," said Poirot, with a little bow.

I looked at her with interest. Her dark hair was ruffled and gave her an elfin look. There was something elfin about her altogether. The small, vivid face, pansy-shaped, the enormous dark blue eyes, and something else—something haunting and arresting. Was it a hint of recklessness ? There were dark shadows under the eyes.

The terrace on which we were sitting was a little used one. The main terrace where most people sat was just round the corner at a point where the cliff shelved directly down to the sea.

From round this corner now there appeared a man, a red-faced man with a rolling carriage who carried his hands half clenched by his side. There was something breezy and care-free about him—a typical sailor.

" I can't think where the girl's got to," he was saying in tones that easily carried to where we sat. " Nick—Nick."

Miss Buckley rose.

" I knew they'd be getting in a state. Attaboy—George—here I am."

" Freddie's frantic for a drink. Come on, girl."

He cast a glance of frank curiosity at Poirot, who must have differed considerably from most of Nick's friends.

The girl performed a wave of introduction.

" This is Commander Challenger—er——"

But to my surprise Poirot did not supply the name for which she was waiting. Instead he rose, bowed very ceremoniously and murmured.

" Of the English Navy. I have a great regard for the English Navy."

This type of remark is not one that an Englishman acclaims most readily. Commander Challenger flushed and Nick Buckley took command of the situation.

"Come on, George. Don't gape. Let's find Freddie and Jim."

She smiled at Poirot.

"Thanks for the cocktail. I hope the ankle will be all right."

With a nod to me she slipped her hand through the sailor's arm and they disappeared round the corner together.

"So that is one of Mademoiselle's friends," murmured Poirot thoughtfully. "One of her cheery crowd. What about him? Give me your expert judgment, Hastings. Is he what you call a good fellow—yes?"

Pausing for a moment to try and decide exactly what Poirot thought I should mean by a "good fellow," I gave a doubtful assent.

"He seems all right—yes," I said. "So far as one can tell by a cursory glance."

"I wonder," said Poirot.

The girl had left her hat behind. Poirot stooped to pick it up and twirled it round absent-mindedly on his finger.

"Has he a *tendresse* for her? What do you think, Hastings?"

"My dear Poirot! How *can* I tell? Here—give me that hat. The lady will want it. I'll take it to her."

Poirot paid no attention to my request. He continued to revolve the hat slowly on his finger.

"*Pas encore. Ça m'amuse.*"

"Really, Poirot!"

" Yes, my friend, I grow old and childish, do I not ? "

This was so exactly what I was feeling that I was somewhat disconcerted to have it put into words. Poirot gave a little chuckle, then leaning forward he laid a finger against the side of his nose.

" But no—I am not so completely imbecile as you think ! We will return the hat—but assuredly—but later ! We will return it to End House and thus we shall have the opportunity of seeing the charming Miss Nick again."

" Poirot," I said. " I believe you have fallen in love."

" She is a pretty girl—eh ? "

" Well—you saw for yourself. Why ask me ? "

" Because, alas ! I cannot judge. To me, nowadays, anything young is beautiful. *Jeunesse— jeunesse*. . . . It is the tragedy of my years. But you—I appeal to you ? Your judgment is not up-to-date, naturally, having lived in the Argentine so long. You admire the figure of five years ago, but you are at any rate more modern than I am. She is pretty— yes ? She has the appeal to the sexes ? "

" One sex is sufficient, Poirot. The answer, I should say, is very much in the affirmative. Why are you so interested in the lady ? "

" Am I interested ? "

" Well—look at what you've just been saying."

" You are under a misapprehension, *mon ami*. I may be interested in the lady—yes—but I am much more interested in her hat."

I stared at him, but he appeared perfectly serious. He nodded his head at me.

" Yes, Hastings, this very hat." He held it towards me. " You see the reason for my interest ? "

" It's a nice hat," I said, bewildered. " But quite an ordinary hat. Lots of girls have hats like it."

" Not like this one."

I looked at it more closely.

" You see, Hastings ? "

" A perfectly plain fawn felt. Good style——"

" I did not ask you to describe the hat. It is plain that you do *not* see. Almost incredible, my poor Hastings, how you hardly ever *do* see ! It amazes me every time anew ! But regard, my dear old imbecile —it is not necessary to employ the grey cells—the eyes will do. Regard—regard——"

And then at last I saw to what he had been trying to draw my attention. The slowly turning hat was revolving on his finger, and that finger was stuck neatly through a hole in the brim of the hat. When he saw that I had realised his meaning, he drew his finger out and held the hat towards me. It was a small neat hole, quite round, and I could not imagine its purpose, if purpose it had.

" Did you observe the way Mademoiselle Nick flinched when a bee flew past ? The bee in the bonnet—the hole in the hat."

" But a bee couldn't make a hole like that."

" Exactly, Hastings ! What acumen ! It could not. *But a bullet could, mon cher* ! "

" *A bullet ?* "

" *Mais oui !* A bullet like *this*."

He held out his hand with a small object in the palm of it.

" A spent bullet, *mon ami*. It was that which hit the terrace just now when we were talking. A spent bullet ! "

" You mean——? "

" *I mean that one inch of difference and that hole would be not through the hat but through the head.* Now do you see why I am interested, Hastings ? You were right, my friend, when you told me not to use the word ' impossible.' Yes—one is human ! Ah ! but he made a grave mistake, that would-be murderer, when he shot at his victim within a dozen yards of Hercule Poirot ! For him, it is indeed *la mauvaise chance.* But you see now why we must make our entry into End House and get into touch with Mademoiselle ? *Three near escapes from death in three days.* That is what she said. We must act quickly, Hastings. The peril is very close at hand."

CHAPTER II

END HOUSE

" Poirot," I said. " I have been thinking."

" An admirable exercise, my friend. Continue it."

We were sitting facing each other at lunch at a small table in the window.

" This shot must have been fired quite close to us. And yet we did not hear it."

" And you think that in the peaceful stillness, with the rippling waves the only sound, we should have done so ? "

" Well, it's odd."

" No, it is not odd. Some sounds—you get used to them so soon that you hardly notice they are there. All this morning, my friend, speedboats have been making trips in the bay. You complained at first—soon, you did not even notice. But, *ma foi*, you could fire a machine gun almost and not notice it when one of those boats is on the sea."

" Yes, that's true."

" Ah ! *voilà*," murmured Poirot. " Mademoiselle and her friends. They are to lunch here, it seems. And therefore I must return the hat. But no matter. The affair is sufficiently serious to warrant a visit all on its own."

He leaped up nimbly from his seat, hurried across the room, and presented the hat with a bow just as

24

Miss Buckley and her companions were seating themselves at table.

They were a party of four, Nick Buckley, Commander Challenger, another man and another girl. From where we sat we had a very imperfect view of them. From time to time the naval man's laugh boomed out. He seemed a simple, likeable soul, and I had already taken a fancy to him.

My friend was silent and distrait during our meal. He crumbled his bread, made strange little ejaculations to himself and straightened everything on the table. I tried to talk, but meeting with no encouragement soon gave it up.

He continued to sit on at the table long after he had finished his cheese. As soon as the other party had left the room, however, he too rose to his feet. They were just settling themselves at a table in the lounge when Poirot marched up to them in his most military fashion, and addressed Nick directly.

" Mademoiselle, may I crave one little word with you."

The girl frowned. I realised her feelings clearly enough. She was afraid that this queer little foreigner was going to be a nuisance. I could not but sympathise with her, knowing how it must appear in her eyes. Rather unwillingly, she moved a few steps aside.

Almost immediately I saw an expression of surprise pass over her face at the low hurried words Poirot was uttering.

In the meantime, I was feeling rather awkward and ill at ease. Challenger with ready tact came to my rescue, offering me a cigarette and making some commonplace observation. We had taken each other's measure and were inclined to be sympathetic to each other. I fancied that I was more his own kind than the man with whom he had been lunching. I now had the opportunity of observing the latter. A tall, fair, rather exquisite young man, with a rather fleshy nose and over-emphasised good-looks. He had a supercilious manner and a tired drawl. There was a sleekness about him that I especially disliked.

Then I looked at the woman. She was sitting straight opposite me in a big chair and had just thrown off her hat. She was an unusual type—a weary Madonna describes it best. She had fair, almost colourless hair, parted in the middle and drawn straight down over her ears to a knot in the neck. Her face was dead white and emaciated—yet curiously attractive. Her eyes were very light grey with large pupils. She had a curious look of detachment. She was staring at me. Suddenly she spoke.

" Sit down—till your friend has finished with Nick."

She had an affected voice, languid and artificial— yet which had withal a curious attraction—a kind of resonant lingering beauty. She impressed me, I think, as the most tired person I had ever met. Tired in mind, not in body, as though she had found everything in the world to be empty and valueless.

" Miss Buckley very kindly helped my friend when he twisted his ankle this morning," I explained, as I accepted her offer.

" So Nick said." Her eyes considered me, still

detachedly. " Nothing wrong with his ankle now, is there ? "

I felt myself blushing.

" Just a momentary sprain," I explained.

" Oh ! well—I'm glad to hear Nick didn't invent the whole thing. She's the most heaven-sent little liar that ever existed, you know. Amazing—it's quite a gift."

I hardly knew what to say. My discomfiture seemed to amuse her.

" She's one of my oldest friends," she said, " and I always think loyalty's such a tiresome virtue, don't you ?   Principally practised by the Scots—like thrift and keeping the Sabbath. But Nick is a liar, isn't she, Jim ? That marvellous story about the brakes of the car—and Jim says there was nothing in it at all."

The fair man said in a soft, rich voice :

" I know something about cars."

He half turned his head. Outside amongst other cars was a long, red car. It seemed longer and redder than any car could be. It had a long gleaming bonnet of polished metal. A super car !

" Is that your car ? " I asked on a sudden impluse.

He nodded.

" Yes."

I had an insane desire to say, " It would be ! "

Poirot rejoined us at that moment. I rose, he took me by the arm, gave a quick bow to the party, and drew me rapidly away.

" It is arranged, my friend. We are to call on Mademoiselle at End House at half-past six. She will be returned from the motoring by then. Yes, yes, surely she will have returned—in safety."

His face was anxious and his tone was worried.

" What did you say to her ? "

" I asked her to accord me an interview—as soon as possible. She was a little unwilling—naturally. She thinks—I can see the thoughts passing through her mind : ' Who is he—this little man ? Is he the bounder, the upstart, the Moving Picture director ? ' If she could have refused she would—but it is difficult —asked like that on the spur of the moment it is easier to consent. She admits that she will be back by six-thirty. *Ça y est* ! "

I remarked that that seemed to be all right then, but my remark met with little favour. Indeed Poirot was as jumpy as the proverbial cat. He walked about our sitting-room all the afternoon, murmuring to himself and ceaselessly rearranging and straightening the ornaments. When I spoke to him, he waved his hands and shook his head.

In the end we started out from the hotel at barely six o'clock.

" It seems incredible," I remarked, as we descended the steps of the terrace. " To attempt to shoot anyone in a hotel garden. Only a madman would do such a thing."

" I disagree with you. Given one condition, it would be quite a reasonably safe affair. To begin with the garden is deserted. The people who come to hotels are like a flock of sheep. It is customary to sit on the terrace overlooking the bay—*eh bien*, so everyone sits on the terrace. Only, I who am an original, sit overlooking the garden. And even then, I *saw* nothing. There is plenty of cover, you observe—trees, groups of palms, flowering shrubs. Anyone could hide himself comfortably and be unobserved whilst he waited for Mademoiselle to pass this way. And she would come this way. To come round by the road from End House would be much longer. Mademoiselle Nick Buckley, she would be of those who are always late and taking the short cut ! "

" All the same, the risk was enormous. He might have been seen—and you can't make shooting look like an accident."

" Not like an *accident*—no."

" What do you mean ? "

" Nothing—a little idea. I may or may not be justified. Leaving it aside for a moment, there is what I mentioned just now—an essential *condition*."

" Which is ? "

" Surely you can tell me, Hastings."

" I wouldn't like to deprive you of the pleasure of being clever at my expense ! "

" Oh ! the sarcasm ! The irony ! Well, what leaps to the eye is this : *the motive cannot be obvious.* If it *were*—why, then, truly the risk would indeed be too great to be taken ! People would say : ' I wonder if it were So-and-So. Where was So-and-So when the shot was fired ? ' No, the murderer—the would-be murderer, I should say—cannot be obvious. And that, Hastings, is why I am afraid ! Yes, at this minute I am afraid. I reassure myself. I say : ' There are four of them.' I say : ' Nothing can happen when they are all together.' I say : ' It would be madness ! '

And all the time I am afraid. These ' accidents '—I want to hear about them ! "

He turned back abruptly.

" It is still early. We will go the other way by the road. The garden has nothing to tell us. Let us inspect the orthodox approach to End House."

Our way led out of the front gate of the hotel and up a sharp hill to the right. At the top of it was a small lane with a notice on the wall : " To End House Only."

We followed it and after a few hundred yards the lane gave an abrupt turn and ended in a pair of dilapidated entrance gates, which would have been the better for a coat of paint.

Inside the gates, to the right, was a small lodge. This lodge presented a piquant contrast to the gates and to the condition of the grass-grown drive. The small garden round it was spick and span, the window frames and sashes had been lately painted and there were clean bright curtains at the windows.

Bending over a flower-bed was a man in a faded Norfolk jacket. He straightened up as the gate creaked and turned to look at us. He was a man of about sixty, six foot at least, with a powerful frame and a weather-beaten face. His head was almost completely bald. His eyes were a vivid blue and twinkled. He seemed a genial soul.

" Good-afternoon," he observed as we passed.

I responded in kind, and as we went on up the drive I was conscious of those blue eyes raking our backs inquisitively.

" I wonder," said Poirot, thoughtfully.

He left it at that without vouchsafing any explanation of what it was that he wondered.

The house itself was large and rather dreary-looking. It was shut in by trees, the branches of which actually touched the roof. It was clearly in bad repair. Poirot swept it with an appraising glance before ringing the bell—an old-fashioned bell that needed a Herculean pull to produce any affect and which once started, echoed mournfully on and on.

The door was opened by a middle-aged woman— " a decent woman in black "—so I felt she should be described. Very respectable, rather mournful, completely uninterested.

Miss Buckley, she said, had not yet returned. Poirot explained that we had an appointment. He had some little difficulty in gaining his point, she was the type that is apt to be suspicious of foreigners. Indeed I flatter myself that it was *my* appearance which turned the scale. We were admitted and ushered into the drawing-room to await Miss Buckley's return.

There was no mournful note here. The room gave on the sea and was full of sunshine. It was shabby and betrayed conflicting styles—ultra modern of a cheap variety superimposed on solid Victorian. The curtains were of faded brocade, but the covers were new and gay and the cushions were positively hectic. On the walls were hung family portraits. Some of them, I thought, looked remarkably good. There was a gramophone and some records lying idly about. There was a portable wireless, practically no books, and one newspaper flung open on the end of the sofa.

Poirot picked it up—then laid it down with a grimace. It was the St. Loo *Weekly Herald and Directory*. Something impelled him to pick it up a second time, and he was glancing at a column when the door opened and Nick Buckley came into the room.

" Bring the ice, Ellen," she called over her shoulder, then addressed herself to us.

" Well, here I am—and I've shaken off the others. I'm devoured with curiosity. Am I the long-lost heroine that is badly wanted for the Talkies ? You were so very solemn "—she addressed herself to Poirot—" that I feel it can't be anything else. Do make me a handsome offer."

" Alas ! Mademoiselle——" began Poirot.

" Don't say it's the opposite," she begged him. " Don't say you paint miniatures and want me to buy one. But no—with that moustache and staying at the Majestic, which has the nastiest food and the highest prices in England—no, it simply can't be."

The woman who had opened the door to us came into the room with ice and a tray of bottles. Nick mixed cocktails expertly, continuing to talk. I think at last Poirot's silence (so unlike him) impressed itself upon her. She stopped in the very act of filling the glasses and said sharply :

" Well ? "

" That is what I wish it to be—well, Mademoiselle." He took the cocktail from her hand. " To your good health, Mademoiselle—to your continued good health."

The girl was no fool. The significance of his tone was not lost on her.

" Is—anything the matter ? "

" Yes, Mademoiselle. This . . ."

He held out his hand to her with the bullet on the palm of it. She picked it up with a puzzled frown.

" You know what that is ? "

" Yes, of course I know. It's a bullet."

" Exactly. Mademoiselle—it was not a wasp that flew past your face this morning—it was this bullet."

" Do you mean—was some criminal idiot shooting bullets in a hotel garden ? "

" It would seem so."

" Well, I'm damned," said Nick frankly. " I do seem to bear a charmed life. That's number four."

" Yes," said Poirot. " That is number four. I want, Mademoiselle, to hear about the other three—accidents."

She stared at him.

" I want to be very sure, Mademoiselle, that they were—*accidents*."

" Why, of course ! What else could they be ? "

" Mademoiselle, prepare yourself, I beg, for a great shock. What if someone is attempting your life ? "

All Nick's response to this was a burst of laughter. The idea seemed to amuse her hugely.

" What a marvellous idea ! My dear man, who on earth do you think would attempt my life ? I'm not the beautiful young heiress whose death releases millions. I wish somebody *was* trying to kill me—that *would* be a thrill, if you like—but I'm afraid there's not a hope ! "

" Will you tell me, Mademoiselle, about those accidents ? "

c

" Of course—but there's nothing in it. They were just stupid things. There's a heavy picture hangs over my bed. It fell in the night. Just by pure chance I had happened to hear a door banging somewhere in the house and went down to find it and shut it—and so I escaped. It would probably have bashed my head in. That's No. 1."

Poirot did not smile.

" Continue, Mademoiselle. Let us pass to No. 2."

" Oh, that's weaker still. There's a scrambly cliff path down to the sea. I go down that way to bathe. There's a rock you can dive off, A boulder got dislodged somehow and came roaring down just missing me. The third thing was quite different. Something went wrong with the brakes of the car—I don't know quite what—the garage man explained, but I didn't follow it. Anyway if I'd gone through the gate and down that hill, they wouldn't have held and I suppose I'd have gone slap into the Town Hall and there would have been the devil of a smash. Slight defacement of the Town Hall, complete obliteration of Me. But owing to my *always* leaving something behind, I turned back and merely ran into the laurel hedge."

" And you cannot tell me what the trouble was ? "

" You can go and ask them at Mott's Garage. They'll know. It was something quite simple and mechanical that had been unscrewed, I think. I wondered if Ellen's boy (my stand-by who opened the door to you, has got a small boy) had tinkered with it. Boys do like messing about with cars. Of course Ellen swore he'd never been near the car. I think something must just have worked loose in spite of what Mott said."

"Where is your garage, Mademoiselle ? "

"Round the other side of the house."

"Is it kept locked ? "

Nick's eyes widened in surprise.

"Oh ! *no*. Of course not."

"Anyone could tamper with the car unobserved?"

"Well—yes—I suppose so. But it's so silly."

"No, Mademoiselle. It is not silly. You do not understand. You are in danger—grave danger. I tell it to you. I ! And you do not know who I am ? "

"No ? " said Nick, breathlessly.

"I am Hercule Poirot."

"Oh ! " said Nick, in rather a flat tone. "Oh, yes."

"You know my name, eh ? "

"Oh, yes."

She wriggled uncomfortably. A hunted look came into her eyes. Poirot observed her keenly.

"You are not at ease. That means, I suppose, that you have not read my books."

"Well—no—not all of them. But I know the name, of course."

"Mademoiselle, you are a polite little liar." (I started, remembering the words spoken at the Majestic Hotel that day after lunch.) "I forget— you are only a child—you would not have heard. So quickly does fame pass. My friend there—he will tell you."

Nick looked at me. I cleared my throat, somewhat embarrassed.

" Monsieur Poirot is—er—was—a great detective,"
I explained.

" Ah ! my friend," cried Poirot. " Is that all you
can find to say ? *Mais dis donc !* Say then to
Mademoiselle that I am a detective unique, unsur-
passed, the greatest that ever lived ! "

" That is now unnecessary," I said coldly. " You
have told her yourself."

" Ah, yes, but it is more agreeable to have been
able to preserve the modesty. One should not sing
one's own praises."

" One should not keep a dog and have to bark
oneself," agreed Nick, with mock sympathy. " Who
is the dog, by the way ? Dr. Watson, I presume."

" My name is Hastings," I said coldly.

" Battle of—1066," said Nick. " Who said I wasn't
educated ? Well, this is all too, *too* marvellous ! Do
you think someone really wants to do away with
me ? It would be thrilling. But, of course, that sort of
thing doesn't really happen. Only in books. I expect
Monsieur Poirot is like a surgeon who's invented an
operation or a doctor who's found an obscure disease
and wants everyone to have it."

" *Sacré tonnerre !* " thundered Poirot. " Will you
be serious ? You young people of to-day, will nothing
make you serious ? It would not have been a joke,
Mademoiselle, if you had been lying in the hotel
garden a pretty little corpse with a nice little hole
through your head instead of your hat. You would
not have laughed then—eh ? "

" Unearthly laughter heard at a *séance*," said Nick.
" But seriously, M. Poirot—it's very kind of you

and all that—but the whole thing *must* be an accident."

" You are as obstinate as the devil ! "

" That's where I got my name from. My grandfather was popularly supposed to have sold his soul to the devil. Everyone round here called him Old Nick. He was a wicked old man—but great fun. I adored him. I went everywhere with him and so they called us Old Nick and Young Nick. My real name is Magdala."

" That is an uncommon name."

" Yes, it's a kind of family one. There have been lots of Magdalas in the Buckley family. There's one up there." She nodded at a picture on the wall.

" Ah ! " said Poirot. Then looking at a portrait hanging over the mantelpiece, he said :

" Is that your grandfather, Mademoiselle ? "

" Yes, rather an arresting portrait, isn't it ? Jim Lazarus offered to buy it, but I wouldn't sell. I've got an affection for Old Nick."

" Ah ! " Poirot was silent for a minute, then he said very earnestly :

" *Revenons à nos moutons.* Listen, Mademoiselle. I implore you to be serious. You are in danger. To-day, somebody shot at you with a Mauser pistol——"

" A Mauser pistol ? "

For the moment she was startled.

" Yes, why ? Do you know of anyone who has a Mauser pistol ? "

She smiled.

" I've got one myself."

" You have ? "

" Yes—it was Dad's. He brought it back from the War. It's been knocking round here ever since. I saw it only the other day in that drawer."

She indicated an old-fashioned bureau. Now, as though suddenly struck by an idea, she crossed to it and pulled the drawer open. She turned rather blankly. Her voice held a new note.

" Oh ! " she said. " It's—it's gone."

CHAPTER III

ACCIDENTS ?

IT was from that moment that the conversation took on a different tone. Up to now, Poirot and the girl had been at cross-purposes. They were separated by a gulf of years. His fame and reputation meant nothing to her—she was of the generation that knows only the great names of the immediate moment. She was, therefore, unimpressed by his warnings. He was to her only a rather comic elderly foreigner with an amusingly melodramatic mind.

And this attitude baffled Poirot. To begin with, his vanity suffered. It was his constant dictum that all the world knew Hercule Poirot. Here was someone who did not. Very good for him, I could not but feel—but not precisely helpful to the object in view !

With the discovery of the missing pistol, however, the affair took on a new phase. Nick ceased to treat it as a mildly amusing joke. She still treated the matter lightly, because it was her habit and her creed to treat all occurrences lightly, but there was a distinct difference in her manner.

She came back and sat down on the arm of a chair, frowning thoughtfully.

" That's odd," she said.

Poirot whirled round on me.

" You remember, Hastings, the little idea I mentioned ? Well, it was correct, my little idea ! Supposing Mademoiselle had been found shot lying in the hotel garden ? She might not have been found for some hours—few people pass that way. And *beside her hand*—just fallen from it—*is her own pistol*. Doubtless the good Madame Ellen would identify it. There would be suggestions, no doubt, of worry or of sleeplessness——"

Nick moved uneasily.

" That's true I have been worried to death. Everybody's been telling me I'm nervy. Yes—they'd say all that. . . ."

" And bring in a verdict of suicide. Mademoiselle's fingerprints conveniently on the pistol and nobody else's—but yes, it would be very simple and convincing."

" How terribly amusing ! " said Nick, but not, I was glad to note, as though she were terribly amused.

Poirot accepted her words in the conventional sense in which they were uttered.

" *N'est ce pas ?* But you understand, Mademoiselle, there must be no more of this. Four failures—yes—but the fifth time there may be a success."

" Bring out your rubber-tyred hearses," murmured Nick.

" But we are here, my friend and I, to obviate all that ! "

I felt grateful for the " we." Poirot has a habit of sometimes ignoring my existence.

" Yes," I put in. " You mustn't be alarmed, Miss Buckley. We will protect you."

" How frightfully nice of you," said Nick. " I think the whole thing is perfectly marvellous. Too, too thrilling."

She still preserved her airy detached manner, but her eyes, I thought, looked troubled.

" And the first thing to do," said Poirot, " is to have the consultation."

He sat down and beamed upon her in a friendly manner.

" To begin with, Mademoiselle, a conventional question—but—have you any enemies ? "

Nick shook her head rather regretfully.

" I'm afraid not," she said, apologetically.

" *Bon*. We will dismiss that possibility then. And now we ask the question of the cinema, of the detective novel—Who profits by your death, Mademoiselle ? "

" I can't imagine," said Nick. " That's why it all seems such nonsense. There's this beastly old barn, of course, but it's mortgaged up to the hilt, the roof leaks and there can't be a coal mine or anything exciting like that hidden in the cliff."

" It is mortgaged—*hein* ? "

" Yes. I had to mortgage it. You see there were two lots of death duties—quite soon after each other. First my grandfather died—just six years ago, and then my brother. That just about put the lid on the financial position."

" And your father ? "

" He was invalided home from the War, then got pneumonia and died in 1919. My mother died when I was a baby. I lived here with grandfather. He and

Dad didn't get on (I don't wonder), so Dad found it convenient to park me and go roaming the world on his own account. Gerald—that was my brother—didn't get on with grandfather either. I dare say I shouldn't have got on with him if I'd been a boy. Being a girl saved me. Grandfather used to say I was a chip of the old block and had inherited his spirit." She laughed. " He was an awful old rip, I believe. But frightfully lucky. There was a saying round here that everything he touched turned to gold. He was a gambler, though, and gambled it away again. When he died he left hardly anything beside the house and land. I was sixteen when he died and Gerald was twenty-two. Gerald was killed in a motor accident just three years ago and the place came to me."

" And after you, Mademoiselle ? Who is your nearest relation ? "

" My cousin, Charles. Charles Vyse. He's a lawyer down here. Quite good and worthy but very dull. He gives me good advice and tries to restrain my extravagant tastes."

" He manages your affairs for you—eh ? "

" Well—yes, if you like to put it that way. I haven't many affairs to manage. He arranged the mortgage for me and made me let the lodge."

" Ah !—the lodge. I was going to ask you about that. It is let ? "

" Yes—to some Australians. Croft their name is. Very hearty, you know—and all that sort of thing. Simply oppressively kind. Always bringing up sticks of celery and early peas and things like that. They're shocked at the way I let the garden go. They're rather a nuisance, really – at least he is. Too terribly friendly for words. She's a cripple, poor thing, and lies on a sofa all day. Anyway they pay the rent and that's the great thing."

" How long have they been here ? "

" Oh ! about six months."

" I see. Now, beyond this cousin of yours – on your father's side or your mother's, by the way ? "

" Mother's. My mother was Amy Vyse."

" *Bien !* Now, beyond this cousin, as I was saying, have you any other relatives ? "

" Some very distant cousins in Yorkshire— Buckleys."

" No one else ? "

" No."

" That is lonely."

Nick stared at him.

" Lonely ? What a funny idea. I'm not down here much, you know. I'm usually in London. Relations are too devastating as a rule. They fuss and inter-fere. It's much more fun to be on one's own."

" I will not waste the sympathy. You are a modern, I see, Mademoiselle. Now—your household."

" How grand that sounds ! Ellen's the household. And her husband, who's a sort of gardener—not a very good one. I pay them frightfully little because I let them have the child here. Ellen does for me when I'm down here and if I have a party we get in who and what we can to help. I'm giving a party on Monday. It's Regatta week, you know."

" Monday—and to-day is Saturday. Yes. Yes.

And now, Mademoiselle, your friends—the ones with whom you were lunching to-day, for instance ? "

" Well, Freddie Rice—the fair girl—is practically my greatest friend. She's had a rotten life. Married to a beast—a man who drank and drugged and was altogether a queer of the worst description. She had to leave him a year or two ago. Since then she's drifted round. I wish to goodness she'd get a divorce and marry Jim Lazarus."

" Lazarus ? The art dealer in Bond Street ? "

" Yes. Jim's the only son. Rolling in money, of course. Did you see that car of his ? He's a Jew, of course, but a frightfully decent one. And he's devoted to Freddie. They go about everywhere together. They are staying at the Majestic over the week-end and are coming to me on Monday."

" And Mrs. Rice's husband ? "

" The mess ? Oh ! he's dropped out of everything. Nobody knows where he is. It makes it horribly awkward for Freddie. You can't divorce a man when you don't know where he is."

" *Évidément !* "

" Poor Freddie," said Nick, pensively. " She's had rotten luck. The thing was all fixed once. She got hold of him and put it to him, and he said he was perfectly willing, but he simply hadn't got the cash to take a woman to a hotel. So the end of it all was she forked out—and he took it and off he went and has never been heard of from that day to this. Pretty mean, I call it."

" Good heavens," I exclaimed.

" My friend Hastings is shocked," remarked

Poirot. " You must be more careful, Mademoiselle. He is out of date, you comprehend. He has just returned from those great clear open spaces, etc., and he has yet to learn the language of nowadays."

" Well, there's nothing to get shocked about," said Nick, opening her eyes very wide. " I mean, everybody knows, don't they, that there are such people. But I call it a low-down trick all the same. Poor old Freddie was so damned hard up at the time that she didn't know where to turn."

" Yes, yes, not a very pretty affair. And your other friend, Mademoiselle. The good Commander Challenger ? "

" George ? I've known George all my life—well, for the last five years anyway. He's a good scout, George."

" He wishes you to marry him—eh ? "

" He does mention it now and again. In the small hours of the morning or after the second glass of port."

" But you remain hard-hearted."

" What would be the use of George and me marrying one another ? We've neither of us got a bean. And one would get terribly bored with George. That ' playing for one's side,' ' good old school ' manner. After all, he's forty if he's a day."

The remark made me wince slightly.

" In fact he has one foot in the grave," said Poirot. " Oh ! do not mind me, Mademoiselle. I am a grandpapa—a nobody. And now, tell me more about these accidents. The picture, for instance ? "

" It's been hung up again—on a new cord. You can come and see it if you like."

She led the way out of the room and we followed her. The picture in question was an oil painting in a heavy frame. It hung directly over the bed-head.

With a murmured, " You permit, Mademoiselle," Poirot removed his shoes and mounted upon the bed. He examined the picture and the cord, and gingerly tested the weight of the painting. With an elegant grimace he descended.

" To have that descend on one's head—no, it would not be pretty. The cord by which it was hung, Mademoiselle, was it, like this one, a wire cable ? "

" Yes, but not so thick. I got a thicker one this time."

" That is comprehensible. And you examined the break—the edges were frayed ? "

" I think so—but I didn't notice particularly. Why should I ? "

" Exactly. As you say, why should you ? All the same, I should much like to look at that piece of wire. Is it about the house anywhere ? "

" It was still on the picture. I expect the man who put the new wire on just threw the old one away."

" A pity. I should like to have seen it."

" You don't think it was just an accident after all ? Surely it couldn't have been anything else."

" It may have been an accident. It is impossible to say. But the damage to the brakes of your car—that was not an accident. And the stone that rolled down the cliff—I should like to see the spot where that accident occurred."

Nick took us out in the garden and led us to the cliff edge. The sea glittered blue below us. A rough path led down the face of the rock. Nick described just where the accident occurred and Poirot nodded thoughtfully. Then he asked :

" How many ways are there into your garden, Mademoiselle ? "

" There's the front way—past the lodge. And a tradesman's entrance—a door in the wall half-way up that lane. Then there's a gate just along here on the cliff edge. It leads out on to a zig-zag path that leads up from that beach to the Majestic Hotel. And then, of course, you can go straight through a gap in the hedge into the Majestic garden—that's the way I went this morning. To go through the Majestic garden is a short cut to the town anyway."

" And your gardener—where does he usually work ? "

" Well, he usually potters round the kitchen garden, or else he sits in the potting-shed and pretends to be sharpening the shears."

" Round the other side of the house, that is to say ? "

" So that if anyone were to come in here and dislodge a boulder he would be very unlikely to be noticed."

Nick gave a sudden little shiver.

" Do you—do you really think that is what happened ? " she asked, " I can't believe it somehow. It seems so perfectly futile."

Poirot drew the bullet from his pocket again and looked at it.

" That was not futile, Mademoiselle," he said gently.

" It must have been some madman."

" Possibly. It is an interesting subject of after-dinner conversation—are all criminals really madmen ? There may be a malformation in their little grey cells—yes, it is very likely. That, it is the affair of the doctor. For me—I have different work to perform. I have the innocent to think of, not the guilty—the victim. not the criminal. It is you I am considering now, Mademoiselle, not your unknown assailant. You are young and beautiful, and the sun shines and the world is pleasant, and there is life and love ahead of you. It is all that of which I think, Mademoiselle. Tell me, these friends of yours, Mrs. Rice and Mr. Lazarus—they have been down here, how long ? "

" Freddie came down on Wednesday to this part of the world. She stopped with some people near Tavistock for a couple of nights. She came on here yesterday. Jim has been touring round about, I believe."

" And Commander Challenger ? "

" He's at Devonport. He comes over in his car whenever he can—week-ends mostly."

Poirot nodded. We were walking back to the house. There was a silence, and then he said suddenly :

" Have you a friend whom you can trust, Mademoiselle ? "

" There's Freddie."

" Other than Mrs. Rice."

" Well, I don't know. I suppose I have. Why ? "

" Because I want you to have a friend to stay with you—immediately."

" Oh ! "

Nick seemed rather taken aback. She was silent a moment or two, thinking. Then she said doubtfully :

" There's Maggie. I could get hold of her, I expect."

" Who is Maggie ? "

" One of my Yorkshire cousins. There's a large family of them. He's a clergyman, you know. Maggie's about my age, and I usually have her to stay sometime or other in the summer. She's no fun, though—one of those painfully pure girls, with the kind of hair that has just become fashionable by accident. I was hoping to get out of having her this year."

" Not at all. Your cousin, Mademoiselle, will do admirably. Just the type of person I had in mind."

" All right," said Nick, with a sigh. " I'll wire her. I certainly don't know who else I could get hold of just now. Everyone's fixed up. But if it isn't the Choirboys' Outing or the Mothers' Beanfeast she'll come all right. Though what you expect her to do. . . ."

" Could you arrange for her to sleep in your room?"

" I suppose so."

" She would not think that an odd request ? "

" Oh, no, Maggie never thinks. She just *does*—earnestly, you know. Christian works—with faith and perseverance. All right, I'll wire her to come on Monday."

" Why not to-morrow ? "

D

" With Sunday trains ? She'll think I'm dying if I suggest that. No, I'll say Monday. Are you going to tell her about the awful fate hanging over me ? "

" *Nous verrons.* You still make a jest of it ? You have courage, I am glad to see."

" It makes a diversion anyway," said Nick.

Something in her tone struck me and I glanced at her curiously. I had a feeling that there was something she had left untold. We had re-entered the drawing-room. Poirot was fingering the newspaper on the sofa.

" You read this, Mademoiselle ? " he asked, suddenly.

" The St. Loo *Herald* ? Not seriously. I opened it to see the tides. It gives them every week."

" I see. By the way, Mademoiselle, have you ever made a will ? "

" Yes, I did. About six months ago. Just before my op."

" *Qu'est ce que vous dites ?* Your *op* ? "

" Operation. For appendicitis. Someone said I ought to make a will, so I did. It made me feel quite important."

" And the terms of that will ? "

" I left End House to Charles. I hadn't much else to leave, but what there was I left to Freddie. I should think probably the—what do you call them— liabilities would have exceeded the assets, really."

Poirot nodded absently.

" I will take my leave now. *Au revoir, Mademoiselle.* Be careful."

" What of ? " asked Nick.

" You are intelligent. Yes, that is the weak point
—in which direction are you to be careful ? Who can
say ? But have confidence, Mademoiselle. In a few
days I shall have discovered the truth."

" Until then beware of poison, bombs, revolver
shots, motor accidents and arrows dipped in the
secret poison of the South American Indians,"
finished Nick glibly.

" Do not mock yourself, Mademoiselle," said
Poirot gravely.

He paused as he reached the door.

" By the way," he said. " What price did M.
Lazarus offer you for the portrait of your grandfather ? "

" Fifty pounds."

" Ah ! " said Poirot.

He looked earnestly back at the dark saturnine face
above the mantelpiece.

" But, as I told you, I don't want to sell the old
boy."

" No," said Poirot, thoughtfully. " No, I understand."

CHAPTER IV

" POIROT," I said, as soon as we were out upon the road. " There is one thing I think you ought to know."

" And what is that, *mon ami* ? "

I told him of Mrs. Rice's version of the trouble with the motor.

" *Tiens ! C'est interessant, ça.* There is, of course, a type, vain, hysterical, that seeks to make itself interesting by having marvellous escapes from death and which will recount to you surprising histories that never happened ! Yes, it is well known, that type there. Such people will even do themselves grave bodily injury to sustain the fiction."

" You don't think that——"

" That Mademoiselle Nick is of that type ? No, indeed. You observed, Hastings, that we had great difficulty in convincing her of her danger. And right to the end she kept up the farce of a half-mocking disbelief. She is of her generation, that little one. All the same, it is interesting—what Madame Rice said. Why should she say it ? Why say it even if it were true ? It was unnecessary—almost *gauche.*"

" Yes," I said. " That's true. She dragged it into

the conversation neck and crop—for no earthly reason that I could see."

"That is curious. Yes, that is curious. The little facts that are curious, I like to see them appear. They are significant. They point the way."

"The way—where?"

"You put your finger on the weak spot, my excellent Hastings. Where? Where indeed! Alas, we shall not know till we get there."

"Tell me, Poirot," I said. "Why did you insist on her getting this cousin to stay?"

Poirot stopped and waved an excited forefinger at me.

"Consider," he cried. "Consider for one little moment, Hastings. How are we handicapped! How are our hands tied! To hunt down a murderer after a crime has been committed—*c'est tout simple!* Or at least it is simple to one of my ability. The murderer has, so to speak, signed his name by committing the crime. But here there is no crime—and what is more we do not want a crime. To detect a crime before it has been committed—that is indeed of a rare difficulty.

"What is our first aim? The safety of Mademoiselle. And that is not easy. No, it is not easy, Hastings. We cannot watch over her day and night —we cannot even send a policeman in big boots to watch over her. We cannot pass the night in a young lady's sleeping chamber. The affair bristles with difficulties.

"But we can do one thing. We can make it more difficult for our assassin. We can put Mademoiselle upon her guard and we can introduce a perfectly impartial witness. It will take a very clever man to get round those two circumstances."

He paused, and then said in an entirely different tone of voice :

" But what I am afraid of, Hastings——"

" Yes ? "

" What I am afraid of is—that he *is* a very clever man. And I am not easy in my mind. No, I am not easy at all."

" Poirot," I said. " You're making me feel quite nervous."

" So am I nervous. Listen, my friend, that paper, the St. Loo *Weekly Herald*. It was open and folded back at—where do you think ? A little paragraph which said, ' *Among the guests staying at the Majestic Hotel are M. Hercule Poirot and Captain Hastings.*' Supposing—just supposing that someone had read that paragraph. They know my name—everyone knows my name——"

" Miss Buckley didn't," I said, with a grin.

" She is a scatterbrain—she does not count. A serious man—a criminal—would know my name. And he would be afraid ! He would wonder ! He would ask himself questions. Three times he has attempted the life of Mademoiselle and now Hercule Poirot arrives in the neighbourhood. ' Is that coincidence ? ' he would ask himself. And he would fear that it might *not* be coincidence. What would he do then ? "

" Lie low and hide his tracks," I suggested.

" Yes—yes—or else—if he had real audacity, he

would strike *quickly*—without loss of time. Before I had time to make the inquiries—*pouf*, Mademoiselle is dead. That is what a man of audacity would do."

" But why do you think that somebody read that paragraph other than Miss Buckley ? "

" It was not Miss Buckley who read that paragraph. When I mentioned my name it meant nothing to her. It was not even familiar. Her face did not change. Besides she told us—she opened the paper to look at the tides—nothing else. Well, there was no tide table on that page."

" You think someone in the house——"

" Someone in the house or who had access to it. And that last is easy—the window stands open. Without doubt Miss Buckley's friends pass in and out."

" Have you any idea ? Any suspicion ? "

Poirot flung out his hands.

" Nothing. Whatever the motive, it is, as I predicted, not an obvious one. That is the would-be murderer's security—that is why he could act so daringly this morning. On the face of it, no one seems to have any reason for desiring the little Nick's death. The property ? End House ? That passes to the cousin—but does he particularly want a heavily mortgaged and very dilapidated old house ? It is not even a family place so far as he is concerned. He is not a Buckley, remember. We must see this M. Charles Vyse, certainly, but the idea seems fantastic.

" Then there is Madame—the bosom friend—with her strange eyes and her air of a lost Madonna——"

" You felt that too ? " I asked, startled.

" What is her concern in the business ? She tells

you that her friend is a liar. *C'est gentille, ça !* Why does she tell you ? Is she afraid of something that Nick may say ? Is that something connected with the car ? Or did she use that as an instance, and was her real fear of something else ? Did anyone tamper with the car, and if so, who ? And does she know about it ?

" Then the handsome blond, M. Lazarus. Where does he fit in ? With his marvellous automobile and his money. Can he possibly be concerned in any way ? Commander Challenger——"

" He's all right," I put in quickly. " I'm sure of that. A real pukka sahib."

" Doubtless he has been to what you consider the right school. Happily, being a foreigner, I am free from these prejudices, and can make investigations unhampered by them. But I will admit that I find it hard to connect Commander Challenger with the case. In fact, I do not see that he can be so connected."

" Of course he can't," I said, warmly.

Poirot looked at me meditatively.

" You have an extraordinary effect on me, Hastings. You have so strongly the *flair* in the wrong direction that I am almost tempted to go by it ! You are that wholly admirable type of man, honest, credulous, honourable, who is invariably taken in by any scoundrel. You are the type of man who invests in doubtful oil fields, and non-existent gold mines. From hundreds like you, the swindler makes his daily bread. Ah, well—I shall study this Commander Challenger. You have awakened my doubts."

"My dear Poirot," I cried, angrily. "You are perfectly absurd. A man who has knocked about the world like I have——"

"Never learns," said Poirot, sadly. "It is amazing —but there it is."

"Do you suppose I'd have made a success of my ranch out in the Argentine if I were the kind of credulous fool you make out?"

"Do not enrage yourself, *mon ami*. You have made a great success of it—you and your wife."

"Bella," I said, "always goes by my judgment."

"She is as wise as she is charming," said Poirot. "Let us not quarrel, my friend. See, there ahead of us, it says Mott's Garage. That, I think, is the garage mentioned by Mademoiselle Buckley. A few inquiries will soon give us the truth of that little matter."

We duly entered the place and Poirot introduced himself by explaining that he had been recommended there by Miss Buckley. He made some inquiries about hiring a car for some afternoon drives and from there slid easily into the topic of the damage sustained by Miss Buckley's car not long ago.

Immediately the garage proprietor waxed voluble. Most extraordinary thing he'd ever seen. He proceeded to be technical. I, alas, am not mechanically minded. Poirot, I should imagine, is even less so. But certain facts did emerge unmistakable. The car had been tampered with. And the damage had been something quite easily done, occupying very little time.

"So that is that," said Poirot, as we strolled

away. " The little Nick was right, and the rich
M. Lazarus was wrong. Hastings, my friend, all this
is very interesting."

" What do we do now ? "

" We visit the post office and send off a telegram
if it is not too late."

" A telegram ? " I said hopefully.

" Yes," said Poirot thoughtfully. " A telegram."

The post office was still open Poirot wrote out his
telegram and despatched it. He vouchsafed me no
information as to its contents. Feeling that he
wanted me to ask him, I carefully refrained from
doing so.

" It is annoying that to-morrow is Sunday," he
remarked, as we strolled back to the hotel. " We
cannot now call upon M. Vyse till Monday morning."

"You could get hold of him at his private address."

" Naturally. But that is just what I am anxious
not to do. I would prefer, in the first place, to consult
him professionally and to form my judgment of him
from that aspect."

" Yes," I said thoughtfully. " I suppose that
would be best."

" The answer to one simple little question, for
instance, might make a great difference. If M.
Charles Vyse was in his office at twelve-thirty this
morning, then it was not he who fired that shot in
the garden of the Majestic Hotel."

" Ought we not to examine the *alibis* of the three
at the hotel ? "

" That is much more difficult. It would be easy
enough for one of them to leave the others for a few

minutes, a hasty egress from one of the innumerable
windows—lounge, smoking-room, drawing-room,
writing-room, quickly under cover to the spot where
the girl must pass—the shot fired and a rapid retreat.
But as yet, *mon ami*, we are not even sure that we
have arrived at all the *dramatis personæ* in the drama.
There is the respectable Ellen—and her so far unseen
husband. Both inmates of the house and possibly,
for all we know, with a grudge against our little
Mademoiselle. There are even the unknown Australians at the lodge. And there may be others,
friends and intimates of Miss Buckley's whom she
has no reason for suspecting and consequently has
not mentioned. I cannot help feeling, Hastings, that
there is something *behind* this—*something* that has
not yet come to light. I have a little idea that Miss
Buckley knows more than she told us."

" You think she is keeping something back ? "

" Yes."

" Possibly with an idea of shielding whoever it is ?"

Poirot shook his head with the utmost energy.

" No, no. As far as that goes, she gave me the impression of being utterly frank. I am convinced that
as regards these attempts on her life, she was telling
all she knew. But there is something else—something
that she believes has nothing to do with that at all.
And I should like to know what that something is.
For I—I say it in all modesty—am a great deal more
intelligent than *une petite comme ça*. I, Hercule
Poirot, might see a connection where she sees none.
It might give me the clue I am seeking. For I
announce to you, Hastings, quite frankly and

humbly, that I am as you express it, all on the sea.
Until I can get some glimmering of the *reason* behind
all this, I am in the dark. There must be *something*—
some factor in the case that I do not grasp. What
is it ? *Je me demande ça sans cesse. Qu'est ce que
c'est ?* "

" You will find out," I said, soothingly.

" So long," he said sombrely, " as I do not find
out too late."

CHAPTER V

MR. AND MRS. CROFT

THERE was dancing that evening at the hotel. Nick Buckley dined there with her friends and waved a gay greeting to us.

She was dressed that evening in floating scarlet chiffon that dragged on the floor. Out of it rose her white neck and shoulders and her small impudent dark head.

" An engaging young devil," I remarked.

" A contrast to her friend—eh ? "

Frederica Rice was in white. She danced with a languorous weary grace that was as far removed from Nick's animation as anything could be.

" She is very beautiful," said Poirot suddenly.

" Who ? Our Nick ? "

" No—the other. Is she evil ? Is she good ? Is she merely unhappy ? One cannot tell. She is a mystery. She is, perhaps, nothing at all. But I tell you, my friend, she is an *allumeuse*."

" What do you mean ? " I asked curiously.

He shook his head, smiling.

" You will feel it sooner or later. Remember my words."

Presently to my surprise, he rose. Nick was dancing with George Challenger. Frederica and

Lazarus had just stopped and had sat down at their table. Then Lazarus got up and went away. Mrs. Rice was alone. Poirot went straight to her table. I followed him.

His methods were direct and to the point.

" You permit ? " He laid a hand on the back of a chair then slid into it. " I am anxious to have a word with you while your friend is dancing."

" Yes ? " Her voice sounded cool, uninterested.

" Madame, I do not know whether your friend has told you. If not, I will. To-day her life has been attempted."

Her great grey eyes widened in horror and surprise. The pupils, dilated black pupils, widened too.

" What do you mean ? "

" Mademoiselle Buckley was shot at in the garden of this hotel."

She smiled suddenly—a gentle, pitying, incredulous smile.

" Did Nick tell you so ? "

" No, Madame, I happened to see it with my own eyes. Here is the bullet."

He held it out to her and she drew back a little.

" But, then—but, then——"

" It is no fantasy of Mademoiselle's imagination, you understand. I vouch for that. And there is more. Several very curious accidents have happened in the last few days. You will have heard—no, perhaps you will not. You only arrived yesterday, did you not ? "

" Yes—yesterday."

" Before that you were staying with friends, I understand. At Tavistock."

" Yes."

" I wonder, Madame, what were the names of the friends with whom you were staying."

She raised her eyebrows.

" Is there any reason why I should tell you that ? " she asked, coldly.

Poirot was immediately all innocent surprise.

" A thousand pardons, Madame. I was most *maladroit*. But I myself, having friends at Tavistock, fancied that you might have met them there. . . . Buchanan—that is the name of my friends."

Mrs. Rice shook her head.

" I don't remember them. I don't think I can have met them." Her tone now was quite cordial. " Don't let us talk about boring people. Go on about Nick. Who shot at her ? Why ? "

" I do not know who—*as yet*," said Poirot. " But I shall find out. Oh ! yes, I shall find out. I am, you know, a detective. Hercule Poirot is my name."

" A very famous name."

" Madame is too kind."

She said slowly :

" What do you want me to do ? "

I think she surprised us both there. We had not expected just that.

" I will ask you, Madame, to watch over your friend."

" I will."

" That is all."

He got up, made a quick bow, and we returned to our own table.

" Poirot," I said, " aren't you showing your hand very plainly ? "

" *Mon ami*, what else can I do ? It lacks subtlety, perhaps, but it makes for safety. *I can take no chances.* At any rate one thing emerges plain to see."

" What is that ? "

" *Mrs. Rice was not at Tavistock.* Where was she ? Ah ! but I will find out. Impossible to keep information from Hercule Poirot. See—the handsome Lazarus has returned. She is telling him. He looks over at us. He is clever, that one. Note the shape of his head. Ah ! I wish I knew——"

" What ? " I asked, as he came to a stop.

" What I shall know on Monday," he returned, ambiguously.

I looked at him but said nothing. He sighed.

" You have no longer the curiosity, my friend. In the old days——"

" There are some pleasures," I said, coldly, " that it is good for you to do without."

" You mean—— ? "

" The pleasure of refusing to answer questions."

" *Ah c'est malin.*"

" Quite so."

" Ah, well, well," murmured Poirot. " The strong silent man beloved of novelists in the Edwardian age."

His eyes twinkled with their old glint.

Nick passed our table shortly afterwards. She

detached herself from her partner and swooped down on us like a gaily-coloured bird.

" Dancing on the edge of death," she said lightly

" It is a new sensation, Mademoiselle ? "

" Yes. Rather fun."

She was off again, with a wave of her hand.

" I wish she hadn't said that," I said, slowly. " Dancing on the edge of death. I don't like it."

" I know. It is too near the truth. She has courage, that little one. Yes, she has courage. But unfortunately it is not courage that is needed at this moment. Caution, not courage—*voilà ce qu'il nous faut !* "

The following day was Sunday. We were sitting on the terrace in front of the hotel, and it was about half-past eleven when Poirot suddenly rose to his feet.

" Come, my friend. We will try a little experiment. I have ascertained that M. Lazarus and Madame have gone out in the car and Mademoiselle with them. The coast is clear."

" Clear for what ? "

" You shall see."

We walked down the steps and across a short stretch of grass to where a gate gave on to the zig-zag path leading down to the sea. A couple of bathers were coming up it. They passed us laughing and talking.

When they had gone, Poirot walked to the point where an inconspicuous small gate, rather rusty on its hinges, bore the words in half obliterated letters, " End House. Private." There was no one in sight. We passed quietly through.

E

In another minute we came out on the stretch of lawn in front of the house. There was no one about. Poirot strolled to the edge of the cliff and looked over. Then he walked towards the house itself. The French windows on to the verandah were open and we passed straight into the drawing-room. Poirot wasted no time there. He opened the door and went out into the hall. From there he mounted the stairs, I at his heels. He went straight to Nick's bedroom—sat down on the edge of the bed and nodded to me with a twinkle.

"You see, my friend, how easy it is. No one has seen us come. No one will see us go. We could do any little affair we had to do in perfect safety. We could, for instance, fray through a picture wire so that it would be bound to snap before many hours had passed. And supposing that by chance anyone did happen to be in front of the house and see us coming. Then we would have a perfectly natural excuse—providing that we were known as friends of the house."

"You mean that we can rule out a stranger?"

"That is what I mean, Hastings. It is no stray lunatic who is at the bottom of this. We must look nearer home than that."

He turned to leave the room and I followed him. We neither of us spoke. We were both, I think, troubled in mind.

And then, at the bend of the staircase, we both stopped abruptly. A man was coming up.

He too stopped. His face was in shadow but his attitude was of one completely taken aback. He was the first to speak, in a loud, rather bullying, voice.

"What the hell are you doing here, I'd like to know?"

"Ah!" said Poirot. "Monsieur—Croft, I think?"

"That's my name, but what——"

"Shall we go into the drawing-room to converse? It would be better, I think."

The other gave way, turned abruptly and descended, we following close on his heels. In the drawing-room, with the door shut, Poirot made a little bow.

"I will introduce myself. Hercule Poirot, at your service."

The other's face cleared a little.

"Oh!" he said slowly. "You're the detective chap. I've read about you."

"In the St. Loo *Herald*?"

"Eh? I've read about you way back in Australia. French, aren't you?"

"Belgian. It makes no matter. This is my friend, Captain Hastings."

"Glad to meet you. But look, what's the big idea? What are you doing here? Anything— wrong?"

"It depends what you call—wrong."

The Australian nodded. He was a fine-looking man in spite of his bald head and advancing years. His physique was magnificent. He had a heavy, rather underhung face—a crude face, I called it to myself. The piercing blue of his eyes was the most noticeable thing about him.

" See here," he said. " I came round to bring little Miss Buckley a handful of tomatoes and a cucumber. That man of hers is no good—bone idle—doesn't grow a thing. Lazy hound. Mother and I—why, it makes us mad, and we feel it's only neighbourly to do what we can ! We've got a lot more tomatoes than we can eat. Neighbours should be matey, don't you think ? I came in, as usual, through the window and dumped the basket down. I was just going off again when I heard footsteps and men's voices overhead. That struck me as odd. We don't deal much in burglars round here—but after all it was possible. I thought I'd just make sure everything was all right. Then I met you two on the stairs coming down. It gave me a bit of a surprise. And now you tell me you're a bonza detective. What's it all about ? "

" It is very simple," said Poirot, smiling. " Mademoiselle had a rather alarming experience the other night. A picture fell above her bed. She may have told you of it ? "

" She did. A mighty fine escape."

" To make all secure I promised to bring her some special chain—it will not do to repeat the occurrence, eh ? She tells me she is going out this morning, but I may come and measure what amount of chain will be needed. *Voilà*—it is simple."

He flung out his hands with a childlike simplicity and his most engaging smile.

Croft drew a deep breath.

" So that's all it is ? "

" Yes—you have had the scare for nothing. We are very law-abiding citizens, my friend and I."

" Didn't I see you yesterday ? " said Croft, slowly.
" Yesterday evening it was. You passed our little place."

" Ah ! yes, you were working in the garden and were so polite as to say good-afternoon when we passed."

" That's right. Well—well. And you're the Monsieur Hercule Poirot I've heard so much about. Tell me, are you busy, Mr. Poirot ? Because if not, I wish you'd come back with me now—have a cup of morning tea, Australian fashion, and meet my old lady. She's read all about you in the newspapers."

" You are too kind, M. Croft. We have nothing to do and shall be delighted."

" That's fine."

" You have the measurements correctly, Hastings ? " asked Poirot, turning to me.

I assured him that I had the measurements correctly, and we accompanied our new friend.

Croft was a talker ; we soon realised that. He told us of his home near Melbourne, of his early struggles, of his meeting with his wife, of their combined efforts and of his final good fortune and success.

" Right away we made up our minds to travel," he said. " We'd always wanted to come to the old country. Well, we did. We came down to this part of the world—tried to look up some of my wife's people—they came from round about here. But we couldn't trace any of them. Then we took a trip on the Continent—Paris, Rome, the Italian Lakes, Florence—all those places. It was while we were in Italy that we had the train accident. My poor

wife was badly smashed up. Cruel, wasn't it ? I've
taken her to the best doctors and they all say the
same—there's nothing for it but time—time and
lying up. It's an injury to the spine."

"What a misfortune ! "

"Hard luck, isn't it ? Well, there it was. And
she'd only got one kind of fancy—to come down here.
She kind of felt if we had a little place of our own—
something small—it would make all the difference.
We saw a lot of messy-looking shacks, and then by
good luck we found this. Nice and quiet and tucked
away—no cars passing, or gramophones next door.
I took it right away."

With the last words we had come to the lodge
itself. He sent his voice echoing forth in a loud
" Cooee," to which came an answering " Cooee."

" Come in," said Mr. Croft. He passed through
the open door and up the short flight of stairs to a
pleasant bedroom. There, on a sofa, was a stout
middle-aged woman with pretty grey hair and a
very sweet smile.

" Who do you think this is, mother ? " said Mr.
Croft. " The extra-special, world-celebrated detective, Mr. Hercule Poirot. I brought him right
along to have a chat with you."

" If that isn't too exciting for words," cried Mrs.
Croft, shaking Poirot warmly by the hand. " Read
about that Blue Train business, I did, and you just
happening to be on it, and a lot about your other
cases. Since this trouble with my back, I've read all
the detective stories that ever were, I should think.
Nothing else seems to pass the time away so quick.

Bert, dear, call out to Edith to bring the tea along."

"Right you are, mother."

"She's a kind of nurse attendant, Edith is," Mrs. Croft explained. "She comes along each morning to fix me up. We're not bothering with servants. Bert's as good a cook and a house-parlourman as you'd find anywhere, and it gives him occupation— that and the garden."

"Here we are," cried Mr. Croft, reappearing with a tray. "Here's the tea. This is a great day in our lives, mother."

"I suppose you're staying down here, Mr. Poirot?" Mrs. Croft asked, as she leaned over a little and wielded the tea-pot.

"Why, yes, Madame, I take the holiday."

"But surely I read that you had retired—that you'd taken a holiday for good and all."

"Ah ! Madame, you must not believe everything you read in the papers."

"Well, that's true enough. So you still carry on business ? "

"When I find a case that interests me."

"Sure you're not down here on work ? " inquired Mr. Croft, shrewdly. "Calling it a holiday might be all part of the game."

"You mustn't ask him embarrassing questions, Bert," said Mrs. Croft. "Or he won't come again. We're simple people, Mr. Poirot, and you're giving us a great treat coming here to-day—you and your friend. You really don't know the pleasure you're giving us."

She was so natural and so frank in her gratification that my heart quite warmed to her.

"That was a bad business about that picture," said Mr. Croft.

"That poor little girl might have been killed," said Mrs. Croft, with deep feeling. "She *is* a live wire. Livens the place up when she comes down here. Not much liked in the neighbourhood, so I've heard. But that's the way in these stuck English places. They don't like life and gaiety in a girl. I don't wonder she doesn't spend much time down here, and that long-nosed cousin of hers has no more chance of persuading her to settle down here for good and all than—than—well, I don't know what."

"Don't gossip, Milly," said her husband.

"Aha!" said Poirot. "The wind is in that quarter. Trust the instinct of Madame! So M. Charles Vyse is in love with our little friend?"

"He's silly about her," said Mrs. Croft. "But she won't marry a country lawyer. And I don't blame her. He's a poor stick, anyway. I'd like her to marry that nice sailor—what's his name, Challenger. Many a smart marriage might be worse than that. He's older than she is, but what of that? Steadying—that's what she needs. Flying about all over the place, the Continent even, all alone or with that queer-looking Mrs. Rice. She's a sweet girl, Mr. Poirot—I know that well enough. But I'm worried about her. She's looked none too happy lately. She's had what I call a haunted kind of look. And it worries me! I've got my reasons for being interested in that girl, haven't I, Bert?"

Mr. Croft got up from his chair rather suddenly.

" No need to go into that, Milly," he said. " I wonder, Mr. Poirot, if you'd care to see some snapshots of Australia ? "

The rest of our visit passed uneventfully. Ten minutes later we took our leave.

" Nice people," I said. " So simple and unassuming. Typical Australians."

" You liked them ? "

" Didn't you ? "

" They were very pleasant—very friendly."

" Well, what is it, then ? There's something, I can see."

" They were, perhaps, just a shade too ' typical,' " said Poirot, thoughtfully. " That cry of Cooee—that insistence on showing us snapshots—was it not playing a part just a little too thoroughly ? "

" What a suspicious old devil you are ! "

" You are right, *mon ami*. I am suspicious of everyone—of everything. I am afraid, Hastings—afraid."

CHAPTER VI

A CALL UPON MR. VYSE

POIROT clung firmly to the Continental breakfast. To see me consuming eggs and bacon upset and distressed him—so he always said. Consequently he breakfasted in bed upon coffee and rolls and I was free to start the day with the traditional Englishman's breakfast of bacon and eggs and marmalade.

I looked into his room on Monday morning as I went downstairs. He was sitting up in bed arrayed in a very marvellous dressing-gown.

" *Bon jour*, Hastings. I was just about to ring. This note that I have written, will you be so good as to get it taken over to End House and delivered to Mademoiselle at once."

I held out my hand for it. Poirot looked at me and sighed.

" If only—if only, Hastings, you would part your hair in the middle instead of at the side ! What a difference it would make to the symmetry of your appearance. And your moustache. If you *must* have a moustache, let it be a real moustache—a thing of beauty such as mine."

Repressing a shudder at the thought, I took the note firmly from Poirot's hand and left the room.

I had rejoined him in our sitting-room when word

was sent up to say Miss Buckley had called. Poirot
gave the order for her to be shown up.

She came in gaily enough, but I fancied that the
circles under her eyes were darker than usual. In
her hand she held a telegram which she handed to
Poirot.

" There," she said. " I hope that will please you ! "

Poirot read it aloud.

" Arrive 5.30 to-day. Maggie."

" My nurse and guardian ! " said Nick. " But
you're wrong, you know. Maggie's got no kind of
brains. Good works is about all she's fit for. That
and never seeing the point of jokes. Freddie would
be ten times better at spotting hidden assassins.
And Jim Lazarus would be better still. I never feel
one has got to the bottom of Jim."

" And the Commander Challenger ? "

" Oh ! George ! He'd never see anything till it
was under his nose. But he'd let them have it when
he did see. Very useful when it came to a show-down,
George would be."

She tossed off her hat and went on :

" I gave orders for the man you wrote about to be
let in. It sounds mysterious. Is he installing a
dictaphone or something like that ? "

Poirot shook his head.

" No, no, nothing scientific. A very simple little
matter of opinion, Mademoiselle. Something I wanted
to know."

" Oh, well," said Nick. " It's all great fun, isn't
it ? "

" Is it, Mademoiselle ? " asked Poirot, gently.

She stood for a minute with her back to us, looking out of the window. Then she turned. All the brave defiance had gone out of her face. It was childishly twisted awry, as she struggled to keep back the tears.

" No," she said. " It—it isn't, really. I'm afraid— I'm afraid. Hideously afraid. And I always thought I was brave."

" So you are, *mon enfant*, so you are. Both Hastings and I, we have both admired your courage."

" Yes, indeed," I put in warmly.

" No," said Nick, shaking her head. " I'm not brave. It's—it's the *waiting*. Wondering the whole time if anything more's going to happen. And *how* it'll happen ! And *expecting* it to happen."

" Yes, yes--it is the strain."

" Last night I pulled my bed out into the middle of the room. And I fastened my window and bolted my door. When I came here this morning, I came round by the road. I couldn't—I simply couldn't come through the garden. It's as though my nerve had gone all of a sudden. It's this thing coming on top of everything else."

" What do you mean exactly by that, Mademoiselle ? On top of everything else ? "

There was a momentary pause before she replied.

" I don't mean anything particular. What the newspapers call ' the strain of modern life,' I suppose. Too many cocktails, too many cigarettes—all that sort of thing. It's just that I've got into a ridiculous —sort of—of state."

She had sunk into a chair and was sitting there, her

small fingers curling and uncurling themselves nervously.

" You are not being frank with me, Mademoiselle. There is something."

" There isn't—there really isn't."

" There is something you have not told me."

" I've told you every single smallest thing."

She spoke sincerely and earnestly.

" About these accidents—about the attacks upon you, yes."

" Well—then ? "

" But you have not told me everything that is in your heart—in your life. . . ."

She said slowly :

" Can anyone do that. . . . ? "

" Ah ! then," said Poirot, with triumph. " You admit it ! "

She shook her head. He watched her keenly.

" Perhaps," he suggested, shrewdly. " It is not *your* secret ? "

I thought I saw a momentary flicker of her eyelids. But almost immediately she jumped up.

" Really and truly, M. Poirot, I've told you every single thing I know about this stupid business. If you think I know something about someone else, or have suspicions, you are wrong. It's having *no* suspicions that's driving me mad ! Because I'm not a fool. I can see that if those ' accidents ' weren't accidents, they must have been engineered by somebody very near at hand—somebody who—knows me. And that's what is so awful. Because I haven't the least idea—not the very least—who that somebody might be."

She went over once more to the window and stood looking out. Poirot signed to me not to speak. I think he was hoping for some further revelation, now that the girl's self-control had broken down.

When she spoke, it was in a different tone of voice, a dreamy far-away voice.

" Do you know a queer wish I've always had ? I love End House. I've always wanted to produce a play there. It's got an—an atmosphere of drama about it. I've seen all sorts of plays staged there in my mind. And now it's as though a drama were being acted there. Only I'm not producing it . . . I'm *in* it ! I'm *right* in it ! I am, perhaps, the person who—dies in the first act."

Her voice broke.

" Now, now, Mademoiselle." Poirot's voice was resolutely brisk and cheerful. " This will not do. This is the hysteria."

She turned and looked at him sharply.

" Did Freddie tell you I was hysterical ? " she asked. " She says I am, sometimes. But you mustn't always believe what Freddie says. There are times, you know, when—when she isn't quite herself."

There was a pause, then Poirot asked a totally irrelevant question :

" Tell me, Mademoiselle," he said. " Have you ever received an offer for End House ? "

" To sell it, do you mean ? "

" That is what I meant."

" No."

" Would you consider selling it if you got a good offer ? "

Nick considered for a moment.

" No, I don't think so. Not, I mean, unless it was such a ridiculously good offer that it would be perfectly foolish not to."

" *Précisément.*"

" I don't want to sell it, you know, because I'm fond of it."

" Quite so. I understand."

Nick moved slowly towards the door.

" By the way, there are fireworks to-night. Will you come ? Dinner at eight o'clock. The fireworks begin at nine-thirty. You can see them splendidly from the garden where it overlooks the harbour."

" I shall be enchanted."

" Both of you, of course," said Nick.

" Many thanks," I said.

" Nothing like a party for reviving the drooping spirits," remarked Nick. And with a little laugh she went out.

" *Pauvre enfant,*" said Poirot.

He reached for his hat and carefully flicked an infinitesimal speck of dust from its surface.

" We are going out ? " I asked.

" *Mais oui*, we have legal business to transact, *mon ami.*"

" Of course. I understand."

" One of your brilliant mentality could not fail to do so, Hastings."

The offices of Messrs. Vyse, Trevannion & Wynnard were situated in the main street of the town.

We mounted the stairs to the first floor and entered a room where three clerks were busily writing. Poirot asked to see Mr. Charles Vyse.

A clerk murmured a few words down a telephone, received, apparently, an affirmative reply, and remarking that Mr. Vyse would see us now, he led us across the passage, tapped on a door and stood aside for us to pass in.

From behind a large desk covered with legal papers, Mr. Vyse rose up to greet us.

He was a tall young man, rather pale, with impassive features. He was going a little bald on either temple and wore glasses. His colouring was fair and indeterminate.

Poirot had come prepared for the encounter. Fortunately he had with him an agreement, as yet unsigned, and on some technical points in connection with this, he wanted Mr. Vyse's advice.

Mr. Vyse, speaking carefully and correctly, was soon able to allay Poirot's alleged doubts, and to clear up some obscure points of the wording.

"I am very much obliged to you," murmured Poirot. "As a foreigner, you comprehend, these legal matters and phrasing are most difficult."

It was then that Mr. Vyse asked who had sent Poirot to him.

"Miss Buckley," said Poirot, promptly. "Your cousin, is she not? A most charming young lady. I happened to mention that I was in perplexity and she told me to come to you. I tried to see you on Saturday morning—about half-past twelve—but you were out."

" Yes, I remember. I left early on Saturday."

" Mademoiselle your cousin must find that large house very lonely ? She lives there alone, I understand."

" Quite so."

" Tell me, Mr. Vyse, if I may ask, is there any chance of that property being in the market ? "

" Not the least, I should say."

" You understand, I do not ask idly. I have a reason ! I am in search, myself, of just such a property. The climate of St. Loo enchants me. It is true that the house appears to be in bad repair, there has not been, I gather, much money to spend upon it. Under those circumstances, is it not possible that Mademoiselle would consider an offer ? "

" Not the least likelihood of it." Charles Vyse shook his head with the utmost decision. " My cousin is absolutely devoted to the place. Nothing would induce her to sell, I know. It is, you understand, a family place."

" I comprehend that, but——"

" It is absolutely out of the question. I know my cousin. She has a fanatical devotion to the house."

A few minutes later we were out in the street again.

" Well, my friend," said Poirot. " And what impression did this M. Charles Vyse make upon you ? "

I considered.

" A very negative one," I said at last. " He is a curiously negative person."

" Not a strong personality, you would say ? "

" No, indeed. The kind of man you would never

F

remember on meeting him again. A mediocre person."

" His appearance is certainly not striking. Did you notice any discrepancy in the course of our conversation with him ? "

" Yes," I said slowly, " I did. With regard to the selling of End House."

" Exactly. Would you have described Mademoiselle Buckley's attitude towards End House as one of ' fanatical devotion ' ? "

" It is a very strong term."

" Yes—and Mr. Vyse is not given to using strong terms. His normal attitude—a legal attitude—is to under, rather than over, state. Yet he says that Mademoiselle has a fanatical devotion to the home of her ancestors."

" She did not convey that impression this morning," I said. " She spoke about it very sensibly, I thought. She's obviously fond of the place—just as anyone in her position would be—but certainly nothing more."

" So, in fact, one of the two is lying," said Poirot, thoughtfully.

" One would not suspect Vyse of lying."

" Clearly a great asset if one has any lying to do," remarked Poirot. " Yes, he has quite the air of a George Washington, that one. Did you notice another thing, Hastings ? "

" What was that ? "

" *He was not in his office at half-past twelve on Saturday.*"

CHAPTER VII

TRAGEDY

THE first person we saw when we arrived at End House that evening was Nick. She was dancing about the hall wrapped in a marvellous kimono covered with dragons.

" Oh ! it's only you ! "

" Mademoiselle—I am desolated ! "

" I know. It did sound rude. But you see, I'm waiting for my dress to arrive. They promised—the brutes—promised faithfully ! "

" Ah ! if it is a matter of *la toilette* ! There is a dance to-night, is there not ? "

" Yes. We are all going on to it after the fireworks. That is, I suppose we are."

There was a sudden drop in her voice. But the next minute she was laughing.

" Never give in ! That's my motto. Don't think of trouble and trouble won't come ! I've got my nerve back to-night. I'm going to be gay and enjoy myself."

There was a footfall on the stairs. Nick turned.

" Oh ! here's Maggie. Maggie, here are the sleuths that are protecting me from the secret assassin. Take them into the drawing-room and let them tell you about it."

In turn we shook hands with Maggie Buckley, and, as requested, she took us into the drawing-room. I formed an immediate favourable opinion of her.

It was, I think, her appearance of calm good sense that so attracted me. A quiet girl, pretty in the old-fashioned sense—certainly not smart. Her face was innocent of make-up and she wore a simple, rather shabby, black evening dress. She had frank blue eyes, and a pleasant slow voice.

" Nick has been telling me the most amazing things," she said. " Surely she must be exaggerating ? Who ever would want to harm Nick ? She can't have an enemy in the world."

Incredulity showed strongly in her voice. She was looking at Poirot in a somewhat unflattering fashion. I realised that to a girl like Maggie Buckley, foreigners were always suspicious.

" Nevertheless, Miss Buckley, I assure you that it is the truth," said Poirot quietly.

She made no reply, but her face remained unbelieving.

" Nick seems quite fey to-night," she remarked. " I don't know what's the matter with her. She seems in the wildest spirits."

That word—fey ! It sent a shiver through me. Also, something in the intonation of her voice had set me wondering.

" Are you Scotch, Miss Buckley ? " I asked, abruptly.

" My mother was Scottish," she explained.

She viewed me, I noticed with more approval than she viewed Poirot. I felt that my statement of the case would carry more weight with her than Poirot's would.

" Your cousin is behaving with great bravery," I said. " She's determined to carry on as usual."

" It's the only way, isn't it ? " said Maggie. " I mean—whatever one's inward feelings are—it is no good making a fuss about them. That's only uncomfortable for everyone else." She paused and then added in a soft voice. " I'm very fond of Nick. She's been very good to me always."

We could say nothing more for at that moment Frederica Rice drifted into the room. She was wearing a gown of Madonna blue and looked very fragile and ethereal. Lazarus soon followed her and then Nick danced in. She was wearing a black frock, and round her was wrapped a marvellous old Chinese shawl of vivid lacquer red.

" Hello, people," she said. " Cocktails ? "

We all drank, and Lazarus raised his glass to her.

" That's a marvellous shawl, Nick," he said. " It's an old one, isn't it ? "

" Yes—brought back by Great-Great-Great-Uncle Timothy from his travels."

" It's a beauty—a real beauty. You wouldn't find another to match it if you tried."

" It's warm," said Nick. " It'll be nice when we're watching the fireworks. And it's gay. I—I hate black."

" Yes," said Frederica. " I don't believe I've ever seen you in a black dress before, Nick. Why did you get it ? "

" Oh ! I don't know." The girl flung aside with a

petulant gesture, but I had caught a curious curl of her lips as though of pain. " Why does one do anything ? "

We went in to dinner. A mysterious manservant had appeared—hired, I presume, for the occasion. The food was indifferent. The champagne, on the other hand, was good.

" George hasn't turned up," said Nick. " A nuisance his having to go back to Plymouth last night. He'll get over this evening sometime or other, I expect. In time for the dance, anyway. I've got a man for Maggie. Presentable, if not passionately interesting."

A faint roaring sound drifted in through the window.

" Oh ! curse that speedboat," said Lazarus. " I get so tired of it."

" That's not the speedboat," said Nick. " That's a seaplane."

" I believe you're right."

" Of course I'm right. The sound's quite different."

" When are you going to get your Moth, Nick ? "

" When I can raise the money," laughed Nick.

" And then, I suppose, you'll be off to Australia like that girl—what's her name ? "

" I'd love to——"

" I admire her enormously," said Mrs. Rice, in her tired voice. " What marvellous nerve ! All by herself too."

" I admire all these flying people," said Lazarus. " If Michael Seton had succeeded in his flight round the world he'd have been the hero of the day—and rightly so. A thousand pities he's come to grief. He's the kind of man England can't afford to lose."

" He may still be all right," said Nick.

" Hardly. It's a thousand to one against by now. Poor Mad Seton."

" They always called him Mad Seton, didn't they ? " asked Frederica.

Lazarus nodded.

" He comes of rather a mad family," he said. " His uncle, Sir Matthew Seton who died about a week ago —he was as mad as a hatter."

" He was the mad millionaire who ran bird sanctuaries, wasn't he ? " asked Frederica.

" Yes. Used to buy up islands. He was a great woman-hater. Some girl chucked him once, I believe, and he took to Natural History by way of consoling himself."

" Why do you say Michael Seton is dead ? " persisted Nick. " I don't see any reason for giving up hope—yet ? "

" Of course, you knew him, didn't you ? " said Lazarus. " I forgot."

" Freddie and I met him at Le Touquet last year," said Nick. " He was too marvellous, wasn't he, Freddie ? "

" Don't ask me, darling. He was your conquest, not mine. He took you up once, didn't he ? "

" Yes—at Scarborough. It was simply too wonderful."

" Have you done any flying, Captain Hastings ? " Maggie asked of me in polite conversational tones.

I had to confess that a trip to Paris and back was the extent of my acquaintance with air travel.

Suddenly, with an exclamation, Nick sprang up.

" There's the telephone. Don't wait for me. It's getting late. And I've asked lots of people."

She left the room. I glanced at my watch. It was just nine o'clock. Dessert was brought, and port. Poirot and Lazarus were talking Art. Pictures. Lazarus was saying, were a great drug in the market just now. They went on to discuss new ideas in furniture and decoration.

I endeavoured to do my duty by talking to Maggie Buckley, but I had to admit that the girl was heavy in hand. She answered pleasantly, but without throwing the ball back. It was uphill work.

Frederica Rice sat dreamily silent, her elbows on the table and the smoke from her cigarette curling round her fair head. She looked like a meditative angel.

It was just twenty past nine when Nick put her head round the door.

" Come out of it, all of you ! The animals are coming in two by two."

We rose obediently. Nick was busy greeting arrivals. About a dozen people had been asked. Most of them were rather uninteresting. Nick, I noticed, made a good hostess. She sunk her modernisms and made everyone welcome in an old-fashioned way. Among the guests I noticed Charles Vyse.

Presently we all moved out into the garden to a place overlooking the sea and the harbour. A few chairs had been placed there for the elderly people, but most of us stood. The first rocket flamed to Heaven.

At that moment I heard a loud familiar voice, and turned my head to see Nick greeting Mr. Croft.

" It's too bad," she was saying, " that Mrs. Croft can't be here too. We ought to have carried her on a stretcher or something."

" It's bad luck on poor mother altogether. But she never complains—that woman's got the sweetest nature—Ha ! that's a good one." This as a shower of golden rain showed up in the sky.

The night was a dark one—there was no moon— the new moon being due in three days' time. It was also, like most summer evenings, cold. Maggie Buckley, who was next me, shivered.

" I'll just run in and get a coat," she murmured.

" Let me."

" No, you wouldn't know where to find it."

She turned towards the house. At that moment Frederica Rice's voice called :

" Oh, Maggie, get mine too. It's in my room."

" She didn't hear," said Nick. " I'll get it, Freddie. I want my fur one—this shawl isn't nearly hot enough. It's this wind."

There was, indeed, a sharp breeze blowing off the sea.

Some set pieces started down on the quay. I fell into conversation with an elderly young lady standing next me who put me through a rigorous catechism as to life, career, tastes and probable length of stay.

Bang! A shower of green stars filled the sky. They changed to blue, then red, then silver.

Another and yet another.

" 'Oh!' and then 'Ah!' that is what one says," observed Poirot suddenly close to my ear. " At the end it becomes monotonous, do you not find ? Brrrr! The grass, it is damp to the feet! I shall suffer for this—a chill. And no possibility of obtaining a proper *tisane* ! "

" A chill ? On a lovely night like this ? "

" A lovely night! A lovely night! You say that, because the rain it does not pour down in sheets! Always when the rain does not fall, it is a lovely night. But I tell you, my friend, if there were a little thermometer to consult you would see."

" Well," I admitted. " I wouldn't mind putting on a coat myself."

" You are very sensible. You have come from a hot climate."

" I'll bring yours."

Poirot lifted first one, then the other foot from the ground with a cat-like motion.

" It is the dampness of the feet I fear. Would it, think you, be possible to lay the hands on a pair of goloshes ? "

I repressed a smile.

" Not a hope," I said. " You understand, Poirot, that it is no longer done."

" Then I shall sit in the house," he declared. " Just for the Guy Fawkes show, shall I want only *enrhumer* myself ? And catch, perhaps, a *fluxion de poitrine* ? "

Poirot still murmuring indignantly, we bent our

footsteps towards the house. Loud clapping drifted up to us from the quay below where another set piece was being shown—a ship, I believe, with *Welcome to Our Visitors* displayed across it.

" We are all children at heart," said Poirot, thoughtfully. " *Les Feus D'Artifices*, the party, the games with balls—yes, and even the conjurer, the man who deceives the eye, however carefully it watches—*mais qu'est ce que vous avez* ? "

I had caught him by the arm, and was clutching him with one hand, while with the other I pointed.

We were within a hundred yards of the house, and just in front of us, between us and the open French window, *there lay a huddled figure wrapped in a scarlet Chinese shawl.* . . .

" *Mon Dieu !* " whispered Poirot. " *Mon Dieu . . .* "

CHAPTER VIII

THE FATAL SHAWL

I SUPPOSE it was not more than forty seconds that we stood there, frozen with horror, unable to move, but it seemed like an hour. Then Poirot moved forward, shaking off my hand. He moved stiffly like an automaton.

"It has happened," he murmured, and I can hardly describe the anguished bitterness of his voice. "In spite of everything—in spite of my precautions, it has happened. Ah! miserable criminal that I am, why did I not guard her better. I should have foreseen—yes—I should have foreseen. Not for one instant should I have left her side."

"You mustn't blame yourself," I said.

My tongue stuck to the roof of my mouth, and I could hardly articulate.

Poirot only responded with a sorrowful shake of his head. He knelt down by the body.

And at that moment we received a second shock.

For Nick's voice rang out, clear and gay, and a moment later Nick appeared in the square of the window silhouetted against the lighted room behind.

"Sorry I've been so long, Maggie," she said. "But——"

Then she broke off—staring at the scene before her.

With a sharp exclamation, Poirot turned over the body on the lawn and I pressed forward to see.

I looked down into the dead face of Maggie Buckley.

In another minute Nick was beside us. She gave a sharp cry.

" Maggie—oh ! Maggie—it—it can't——"

Poirot was still examining the girl's body. At last very slowly he rose to his feet.

" Is she—is——" Nick's voice broke off."

" Yes, Mademoiselle. She is dead."

" But why ? But why ? Who could have wanted to kill *her* ? "

Poirot's reply came quickly and firmly.

" It was not her they meant to kill, Mademoiselle ! It was *you* ! They were misled by the shawl."

A great cry broke from Nick.

" Why couldn't it have been me ? " she wailed. " Oh ! why couldn't it have been me ? I'd so much rather. I don't want to live—*now*. I'd be glad—willing—happy—to die."

She flung up her arms wildly and then staggered slightly. I passed an arm round her quickly to support her.

" Take her into the house, Hastings," said Poirot. " Then ring up the police."

" The police ? "

" *Mais oui* ! Tell them someone has been shot. And afterwards stay with Mademoiselle Nick. *On no account leave her*."

I nodded comprehension of these instructions, and supporting the half-fainting girl, made my way through the drawing-room window. I laid the girl on the sofa there, with a cushion under her head, and then hurried out into the hall in search of the telephone.

I gave a slight start on almost running into Ellen. She was standing there with a most peculiar expression on her meek, respectable face. Her eyes were glittering and she was passing her tongue repeatedly over her dry lips. Her hands were trembling, as though with excitement. As soon as she saw me, she spoke.

" Has—has anything happened, sir ? "

" Yes," I said curtly. " Where's the telephone ? "

" Nothing—nothing wrong, sir ? "

" There's been an accident," I said evasively. " Somebody hurt. I must telephone."

" Who has been hurt, sir ? "

There was a positive eagerness in her face.

" Miss Buckley. Miss Maggie Buckley."

" Miss Maggie ? Miss *Maggie* ? Are you sure, sir —I mean are you sure that—that it's Miss Maggie ? "

" I'm quite sure," I said. " Why ? "

" Oh !—nothing. I—I thought it might be one of the other ladies. I thought perhaps it might be— Mrs. Rice."

" Look here," I said. " Where's the telephone ? "

" It's in the little room here, sir." She opened the door for me and indicated the instrument.

" Thanks," I said. And, as she seemed disposed to linger, I added : " That's all I want, thank you."

" If you want Dr. Graham——"

" No, no," I said. " That's all. Go, please."

She withdrew reluctantly, as slowly as she dared. In all probability she would listen outside the door, but I could not help that. After all, she would soon know all there was to be known.

I got the police station and made my report. Then, on my own initiative, I rang up the Dr. Graham Ellen had mentioned. I found his number in the book. Nick, at any rate, should have medical attention, I felt—even though a doctor could do nothing for that poor girl lying out there. He promised to come at once and I hung up the receiver and came out into the hall again.

If Ellen had been listening outside the door she had managed to disappear very swiftly. There was no one in sight when I came out. I went back into the drawing-room. Nick was trying to sit up.

"Do you think—could you get me—some brandy?"

"Of course."

I hurried into the dining-room, found what I wanted and came back. A few sips of the spirit revived the girl. The colour began to come back into her cheeks. I rearranged the cushion for her head.

"It's all—so awful." She shivered. "Everything —everywhere."

"I know, my dear, I know."

"No, you don't ! You can't And it's all such a *waste*. If it only were me. It would be all over. . . ."

"You mustn't," I said, "be morbid."

She only shook her head, reiterating : "You don't know ! You don't *know* !"

Then, suddenly, she began to cry. A quiet, hopeless sobbing like a child. That, I thought, was probably the best thing for her, so I made no effort to stem her tears.

When their first violence had died down a little, I stole across to the window and looked out. I had heard an outcry of voices a few minutes before. They were all there by now, a semi-circle round the scene of the tragedy, with Poirot like a fantastical sentinel, keeping them back.

As I watched, two uniformed figures came striding across the grass. The police had arrived.

I went quietly back to my place by the sofa. Nick lifted her tear-stained face.

" Oughtn't I to be doing something ? "

"No, my dear. Poirot will see to it. Leave it to him."

Nick was silent for a minute or two, then she said :

" Poor Maggie. Poor dear old Maggie. Such a good sort who never harmed a soul in her life. That this should happen to *her*. I feel as though I'd killed her—bringing her down in the way that I did."

I shook my head sadly. How little one can foresee the future. When Poirot insisted on Nick's inviting a friend, how little did he think that he was signing an unknown girl's death warrant.

We sat in silence. I longed to know what was going on outside, but I loyally fulfilled Poirot's instructions and stuck to my post.

It seemed hours later when the door opened and Poirot and a police inspector entered the room. With them came a man who was evidently Dr. Graham. He came over at once to Nick.

" And how are you feeling, Miss Buckley ? This must have been a terrible shock." His fingers were on her pulse. " Not too bad."

He turned to me.

" Has she had anything ? "

" Some brandy," I said.

" I'm all right," said Nick, bravely.

" Able to answer a few questions, eh ? "

" Of course."

The police inspector moved forward with a preliminary cough. Nick greeted him with the ghost of a smile.

" Not impeding the traffic this time," she said.

I gathered they were not strangers to each other.

" This is a terrible business, Miss Buckley," said the inspector. " I'm very sorry about it. Now Mr. Poirot here, whose name I'm very familiar with (and proud we are to have him with us, I'm sure), tells me that to the best of his belief you were shot at in the grounds of the Majestic Hotel the other morning ? "

Nick nodded.

" I thought it was just a wasp," she explained. " But it wasn't."

" And you'd had some rather peculiar accidents before that ? "

" Yes—at least it was odd their happening so close together."

She gave a brief account of the various circumstances.

" Just so. Now how came it that your cousin was wearing your shawl to-night ? "

" We came in to fetch her coat—it was rather cold watching the fireworks. I flung off the shawl on the sofa here. Then I went upstairs and put on the coat I'm wearing now— a light nutria one. I also got a wrap for my friend Mrs. Rice out of her room.

G

There it is on the floor by the window. Then Maggie called out that she couldn't find her coat. I said it must be downstairs. She went down and called up she still couldn't find it. I said it must have been left in the car—it was a tweed coat she was looking for—she hasn't got an evening furry one—and I said I'd bring her down something of mine. But she said it didn't matter—she'd take my shawl if I didn't want it. And I said of course but would that be enough ? And she said Oh, yes, because she really didn't feel it particularly cold after Yorkshire. She just wanted *something*. And I said all right, I'd be out in a minute. And when I did—did come out——"

She stopped, her voice breaking. . . .

" Now, don't distress yourself, Miss Buckley. Just tell me this. Did you hear a shot—or two shots ? "

Nick shook her head.

" No—only just the fireworks popping and the squibs going off."

" That's just it," said the inspector. " You'd never notice a shot with all that going on. It's no good asking you, I suppose, if you've any clue to who it is making these attacks upon you ? "

" I haven't the least idea," said Nick. " I can't imagine."

" And you wouldn't be likely to," said the inspector. " Some homicidal maniac—that's what it looks like to me. Nasty business. Well, I won't need to ask you any more questions to-night, miss. I'm more sorry about this than I can say."

Dr. Graham stepped forward.

" I'm going to suggest, Miss Buckley, that you

don't stay here. I've been talking it over with
M. Poirot. I know of an excellent nursing home.
You've had a shock, you know. What you need is
complete rest——"

Nick was not looking at him. Her eyes had gone
to Poirot.

" Is it—because of the shock ? " she asked.

He came forward.

" I want you to feel safe, *mon enfant*. And *I* want
to feel, too, that you *are* safe. There will be a nurse
there—a nice practical unimaginative nurse. She
will be near you all night. When you wake up and
cry out—she will be there, close at hand. You
understand ? "

" Yes," said Nick, " I understand. But *you* don't.
I'm not afraid any longer. I don't care one way or
another. If any one wants to murder me, they can."

" Hush, hush," I said. " You're over-strung."

" You don't know. None of you know ! "

" I really think M. Poirot's plan is a very good
one," the doctor broke in soothingly. " I will take
you in my car. And we will give you a little something to ensure a good night's rest. Now what do
you say ? "

" I don't mind," said Nick. " Anything you like.
It doesn't matter."

Poirot laid his hand on hers.

" I know, Mademoiselle. I know what you must
feel. I stand before you ashamed and stricken to the
heart. I, who promised protection, have not been
able to protect. I have failed. I am a miserable. But
believe me, Mademoiselle, my heart is in agony

because of that failure. If you knew what I am
suffering you would forgive, I am sure."

"That's all right," said Nick, still in the same dull
voice. "You mustn't blame yourself. I'm sure you
did the best you could. Nobody could have helped
it—or done more, I'm sure. Please don't be unhappy."

"You are very generous, Mademoiselle."

"No, I——"

There was an interruption. The door flew open and
George Challenger rushed into the room.

"What's all this?" he cried. "I've just arrived.
To find a policeman at the gate and a rumour that
somebody's dead. What is it all about? For God's
sake, tell me. Is it—is it—Nick?"

The anguish in his tone was dreadful to hear. I
suddenly realised that Poirot and the doctor between
them completely blotted out Nick from his sight.

Before anyone had time to answer, he repeated
his question.

"Tell me—it can't be true—Nick isn't *dead*?"

"No, *mon ami*," said Poirot, gently. "She is
alive."

And he drew back so that Challenger could see the
little figure on the sofa.

For a moment or two Challenger stared at her
incredulously. Then, staggering a little, like a
drunken man, he muttered :

"Nick—Nick."

And suddenly dropping on his knees beside the
sofa and hiding his head in his hands, he cried in a
muffled voice :

"Nick—my darling—I thought that you were dead."

Nick tried to sit up.

"It's all right, George. Don't be an idiot. I'm quite safe."

He raised his head and looked round wildly.

"But *somebody's* dead? The policeman said so."

"Yes," said Nick. "Maggie. Poor old Maggie. Oh !——"

A spasm twisted her face. The doctor and Poirot came forward. Graham helped her to her feet. He and Poirot, one on each side, helped her from the room.

"The sooner you get to your bed the better," remarked the doctor. "I'll take you along at once in my car. I've asked Mrs. Rice to pack a few things ready for you to take."

They disappeared through the door. Challenger caught my arm.

"I don't understand. Where are they taking her?"

I explained.

"Oh ! I see. Now, then, Hastings, for God's sake give me the hang of this thing. What a ghastly tragedy ! That poor girl."

"Come and have a drink," I said. "You're all to pieces."

"I don't mind if I do."

We adjourned to the dining-room.

"You see," he explained, as he put away a stiff whisky and soda. "I thought it was Nick."

There was very little doubt as to the feelings of Commander George Challenger. A more transparent lover never lived.

CHAPTER IX

A. TO J.

I DOUBT if I shall ever forget the night that followed. Poirot was a prey to such an agony of self-reproach that I was really alarmed. Ceaselessly he strode up and down the room heaping anathemas on his own head and deaf to my well-meant remonstrances.

" What it is to have too good an opinion of oneself. I am punished—yes, I am punished. I, Hercule Poirot. I was too sure of myself."

" No, no," I interpolated.

" But who would imagine—who could imagine—such unparalleled audacity ? I had taken, as I thought, all possible precautions. I had warned the murderer——"

" Warned the murderer ? "

" *Mais oui*. I had drawn attention to myself. I had let him see that I suspected—someone. I had made it, or so I thought, too dangerous for him to dare to repeat his attempts at murder. I had drawn a cordon round Mademoiselle. And he slips through it ! Boldly—under our very eyes almost, he slips through it ! In spite of us all—of everyone being on the alert, he achieves his object."

" Only he doesn't," I reminded him.

" That is the chance only ! From my point of

view, it is the same. A human life has been taken, Hastings—whose life is non-essential."

"Of course," I said. "I didn't mean that."

"But on the other hand, what you say is true. And that makes it worse—ten times worse. For the murderer is still as far as ever from achieving his object. Do you understand, my friend ? The position is changed—for the worse. It may mean that not one life—but two—will be sacrificed."

"Not while you're about," I said stoutly.

He stopped and wrung my hand.

"*Merci, mon ami ! Merci !* You still have confidence in the old one—you still have the faith. You put new courage into me. Hercule Poirot will not fail again. No second life shall be taken. I will rectify my error—for, see you, there must have been an error ! Somewhere there has been a lack of order and method in my usually so well arranged ideas. I will start again. Yes, I will start at the beginning. And this time—I will not fail."

"You really think, then," I said, "that Nick Buckley's life is still in danger ? "

"My friend, for what other reason did I send her to this nursing home ? "

"Then it wasn't the shock——"

"The shock ! Pah ! One can recover from shock as well in one's own home as in a nursing home— better, for that matter. It is not amusing there, the floors of green linoleum, the conversation of the nurses—the meals on trays, the ceaseless washing. No, no, it is for safety and safety only. I take the doctor into my confidence. He agrees. He will make all arrangements. No one, *mon ami, not even her dearest friend*, will be admitted to see Miss Buckley. You and I are the only ones permitted. *Pour les autres—eh bien !* ' Doctor's orders,' they will be told. A phrase very convenient and one not to be gainsayed."

" Yes," I said. " Only——"

" Only what, Hastings ? "

" That can't go on for ever."

" A very true observation. But it gives us a little breathing space. And you realise, do you not, that the character of our operations has changed."

" In what way ? "

" Our original task was to ensure the safety of Mademoiselle. Our task now is a much simpler one —a task with which we are well acquainted. It is neither more nor less than the hunting down of a murderer."

" You call that simpler ? "

" Certainly it is simpler. The murderer has, as I said the other day, *signed his name to the crime*. He has come out into the open."

" You don't think——" I hesitated, then went on. " You don't think that the police are right ? That this is the work of a madman, some wandering lunatic with homicidal mania ? "

" I am more than ever convinced that such is not the case."

" You really think that——"

I stopped. Poirot took up my sentence, speaking very gravely.

" That the murderer is someone in Mademoiselle's own circle ? Yes, *mon ami*, I do."

" But surely last night must almost rule out that possibility. We were all together and——"

He interrupted.

" Could you swear, Hastings, that any particular person had never left our little company there on the edge of the cliff ? Is there any one person there whom you could swear you had seen *all* the time ? "

" No," I said slowly, struck by his words. " I don't think I could. It was dark. We all moved about, more or less. On different occasions I noticed Mrs. Rice, Lazarus, you, Croft, Vyse—but all the time—no."

Poirot nodded his head.

" Exactly. It would be a matter of a very few minutes. The two girls go to the house. The murderer slips away unnoticed, hides behind that sycamore tree in the middle of the lawn. Nick Buckley, or so he thinks, comes out of the window, passes within a foot of him, he fires three shots in rapid succession——"

" Three ? " I interjected.

" Yes. He was taking no chances this time. We found three bullets in the body."

" That was risky, wasn't it ? "

" Less risky in all probability than one shot would have been. A Mauser pistol does not make a great deal of noise. It would resemble more or less the popping of the fireworks and blend in very well with the noise of them."

" Did you find the pistol ? " I asked.

" No. And there, Hastings, lies to my mind the

indisputable proof that no stranger is responsible for this. We agree, do we not, that Miss Buckley's own pistol was taken in the first place for one reason only —to give her death the appearance of suicide."

" Yes."

" That is the only possible reason, is it not ? But now, you observe, there is no pretence of suicide. *The murderer knows that we should not any longer be deceived by it.* He knows, in fact, what we know ! "

I reflected, admitting to myself the logic of Poirot's deduction.

" What did he do with the pistol, do you think ? "

Poirot shrugged his shoulders.

" For that, it is difficult to say. But the sea was exceedingly handy. A good toss of the arm, and the pistol sinks, never to be recovered. We cannot, of course, be absolutely sure—but that is what *I* should have done."

His matter-of-fact tone made me shiver a little.

" Do you think—do you think he realised that he'd killed the wrong person ? "

" I am quite sure he did not," said Poirot, grimly. " Yes, that must have been an unpleasant little surprise for him when he learnt the truth. To keep his face and betray nothing—it cannot have been easy."

At that moment I bethought me of the strange attitude of the maid, Ellen. I gave Poirot an account of her peculiar demeanour. He seemed very interested.

" She betrayed surprise, did she, that it was Maggie who was dead ? "

" Great surprise."

" That is curious. And yet, the fact of a tragedy was clearly *not* a surprise to her. Yes, there is something there that must be looked into. Who is she, this Ellen ? So quiet, so respectable in the English manner ? Could it be she who—— ? " He broke off.

" If you're going to include the accidents," I said, " surely it would take a man to have rolled that heavy boulder down the cliff."

" Not necessarily. It is very largely a question of leverage. Oh, yes, it could be done."

He continued his slow pacing up and down of the room.

" Anyone who was at End House last night comes under suspicion. But those guests—no, I do not think it was one of them. For the most part, I should say, they were mere acquaintances. There was no intimacy between them and the young mistress of the house."

" Charles Vyse was there," I remarked.

" Yes, we must not forget him. He is, logically, our strongest suspect." He made a gesture of despair and threw himself into a chair opposite mine. " *Voilà*— it is always that we come back to ! Motive ! We must find the motive if we are to understand this crime. And it is there, Hastings, that I am continually baffled. Who can possibly have a motive for doing away with Mademoiselle Nick ? I have let myself go to the most absurd suppositions. I, Hercule Poirot, have descended to the most ignominious flights of fancy. I have adopted the mentality of the cheap thriller. The grandfather—the ' Old Nick '— he who is supposed to have gambled his money away.

Did he really do so, I have asked myself ? Did he, on the contrary, hide it away ? Is it hidden somewhere in End House ? Buried somewhere in the grounds ? With that end in view (I am ashamed to say it) I inquired of Mademoiselle Nick whether there had ever been any offers to buy the house."

" Do you know, Poirot," I said. " I call that rather a bright idea. There may be something in it."

Poirot groaned.

" You would say that ! It would appeal, I knew, to your romantic but slightly mediocre mind. Buried treasure—yes, you would enjoy that idea."

" Well—I don't see why not——"

" Because, my friend, the more prosaic explanation is nearly always the more probable. Then Mademoiselle's father—I have played with even more degrading ideas concerning him. He was a traveller. Supposing, I say to myself, that he has stolen a jewel—the eye of a God. Jealous priests are on his tracks. Yes, I, Hercule Poirot, have descended to depths such as these.

" I have had other ideas concerning this father," he went on. " Ideas at once more dignified and more probable. Did he, in the course of his wanderings, contract a second marriage ? Is there a nearer heir than M. Charles Vyse ? But again, that leads nowhere, for we are up against the same difficulty— that there is really nothing of value to inherit.

" I have neglected no possibility. Even that chance reference of Mademoiselle Nick's to the offer made her by M. Lazarus. You remember ? The offer to purchase her grandfather's portrait. I telegraphed on

Saturday for an expert to come down and examine that picture. He was the man about whom I wrote to Mademoiselle this morning. Supposing, for instance, it were worth several thousand pounds ? "

" You surely don't think a rich man like young Lazarus—— ? "

" Is he rich ? Appearances are not everything. Even an old-established firm with palatial showrooms and every appearance of prosperity may rest on a rotten basis. And what does one do then ? Does one run about crying out that times are hard ? No, one buys a new and luxurious car. One spends a little more money than usual. One lives a little more ostentatiously. For credit, see you, is everything ! But sometimes a monumental business has crashed —for no more than a few thousand pounds—*of ready money.*

" Oh ! I know," he continued, forestalling my protests. " It is far-fetched—but it is not so bad as revengeful priests or buried treasure. It bears, at any rate, some relationship to things as they happen. And we can neglect nothing—nothing that might bring us nearer the truth."

With careful fingers he straightened the objects on the table in front of him. When he spoke, his voice was grave and, for the first time, calm.

" *Motive !* " he said. " Let us come back to that, and regard this problem calmly and methodically. To begin with, how many kinds of motive are there for murder ? What are the motives which lead one human being to take another human being's life ?

" We exclude for the moment homicidal mania.

Because I am absolutely convinced that the solution of our problem does not lie there. We also exclude killing done on the spur of the moment under the impulse of an ungovernable temper. This is cold-blooded deliberate murder. What are the motives that actuate such a murder as that ?

" There is, first, *Gain*. Who stood to gain by Mademoiselle Buckley's death ? Directly or indirectly. Well, we can put down Charles Vyse. He inherits a property that, from the financial point of view, is probably not worth inheriting. He might, perhaps, pay off the mortgage, build small villas on the land and eventually make a small profit. It is possible. The place might be worth something to him if he had any deeply cherished love of it—if, it were, for instance, a family place. That is, undoubtedly, an instinct very deeply implanted in some human beings, and it has, in cases I have known, actually led to crime. But I cannot see any such motive in M. Vyse's case.

" The only other person who would benefit at all by Mademoiselle Buckley's death is her friend, Madame Rice. But the amount would clearly be a very small one. Nobody else, as far as I can see, *gains* by Mademoiselle Buckley's death.

" What is another motive ? Hate—or love that has turned to hate. The *crime passionnel*. Well, there again we have the word of the observant Madame Croft that both Charles Vyse and Commander Challenger are in love with the young lady."

" I think we can say that we have observed the

latter phenomenon for ourselves," I remarked, with
a smile.

"Yes—he tends to wear his heart on his sleeve, the
honest sailor. For the other, we rely on the word of
Madame Croft. Now, if Charles Vyse felt that he
were supplanted, would he be so powerfully affected
that he would kill his cousin rather than let her
become the wife of another man ? "

" It sounds very melodramatic," I said, doubtfully.

" It sounds, you would say, un-English. I agree.
But even the English have emotions. And a type,
such as Charles Vyse, is the most likely to have them.
He is a repressed young man. One who does not
show his feelings easily. Such often have the most
violent feelings. I would never suspect the Commander Challenger of murder for emotional reasons.
No, no, he is not the type. But with Charles Vyse—
yes, it is possible. But it does not entirely satisfy me.

" Another motive for crime—Jealousy. I separate
it from the last, because jealousy may not, necessarily, be a sexual emotion. There is envy—envy of
possession—of supremacy. Such a jealousy as drove
the Iago of your great Shakespeare to one of the
cleverest crimes (speaking from the professional
point of view) that has ever been committed."

" Why was it so clever ? " I asked, momentarily
diverted.

" *Parbleu*—because he got others to execute it.
Imagine a criminal nowadays on whom one was
unable to put the handcuffs because he had never
done anything himself. But this is not the subject

we were discussing. Can jealousy, of any kind, be responsible for this crime ? Who has reason to envy Mademoiselle ? Another woman ? There is only Madame Rice, and as far as we can see, there was no rivalry between the two women. But again, that is only ' as far as we can see.' There may be something there.

" Lastly—Fear. Does Mademoiselle Nick, by any chance, hold somebody's secret in her power ? Does she know something which, if it were known, might ruin another life ? If so, I think we can say very definitely, *that she herself is unaware of it*. But that might be, you know. That might be. And if so, it makes it very difficult. Because, whilst she holds the clue in her hands, she holds it unconsciously and will be quite unable to tell us what it is."

" You really think that is possible ? "

" It is a hypothesis. I am driven to it by the difficulty of finding a reasonable theory elsewhere. When you have eliminated other possibilities you turn to the one that is left and say—since the other is not—*this must be so*. . . ."

He was silent a long time.

At last, rousing himself from his absorption, he drew a sheet of paper towards him and began to write.

" What are you writing ? " I asked, curiously.

" *Mon ami*, I am composing a list. It is a list of people surrounding Mademoiselle Buckley. Within that list, if my theory is correct, there must be the name of the murderer."

He continued to write for perhaps twenty minutes

—then shoved the sheets of paper across to me.
" *Voilà, mon ami*. See what you make of it."
The following is a reproduction of the paper:

    A. Ellen.
    B. Her gardener husband.
    C. Their child.
    D. Mr. Croft.
    E. Mrs. Croft.
    F. Mrs. Rice.
    G. Mr. Lazarus.
    H. Commander Challenger.
    I. Mr. Charles Vyse.
    J.

Remarks :

 A. *Ellen.*—Suspicious circumstances. Her attitude
    and words on hearing of the crime. Best
    opportunity of anyone to have staged
    accidents and to have known of pistol, *but*
    unlikely to have tampered with car, and
    general mentality of crime seems above her
    level.

    Motive.—None—unless Hate arising out of
    some incident unknown.

    Note.—Further inquiries as to her antecedents
    and general relations with N. B.

 B. *Her Husband.*—Same as above. More likely to
    have tampered with car.

    Note.—Should be interviewed.

H

C. *Child.*—Can be ruled out.
   Note.—Should be interviewed. Might give valuable information.

D. *Mr. Croft.*—Only suspicious circumstance the fact that we met him mounting the stair to bedroom floor. Had ready explanation which may be true. But it may not !
   Nothing known of antecedents.
   Motive.—None.

E. *Mrs. Croft.*—Suspicious circumstances. None.
   Motive.—None.

F. *Mrs. Rice.*—Suspicious circumstances. Full opportunity. Asked N. B. to fetch wrap. Has deliberately tried to create impression that N. B. is a liar and her account of " accidents " not to be relied on. Was not at Tavistock when accidents occurred. Where was she ?
   Motive.—*Gain ?* Very slight. *Jealousy ?* Possible, but nothing known. *Fear ?* Also possible, but nothing known.
   Note.—Converse with N. B. on subject. See if any light is thrown upon matter. Possibly something to do with F. R.'s marriage.

G. *Mr. Lazarus.* — Suspicious circumstances. General opportunity. Offer to buy picture. Said brakes of car were quite all right

(according to F. R.). May have been in
neighbourhood prior to Friday.

Motive.—None—unless profit on picture. *Fear?*
—unlikely.

Note.—Find out where J. L. was before
arriving at St. Loo. Find out financial
position of Aaron Lazarus & Son.

H. *Commander Challenger.*—Suspicious circumstances. None. Was in neighbourhood all
last week, so opportunity for " accidents "
good. Arrived half an hour after murder.

Motive.—None.

I. *Mr. Vyse.*—Suspicious circumstances. Was
absent from office at time when shot was
fired in garden of hotel. Opportunity good.
Statement about selling of End House open
to doubt. Of a repressed temperament.
Would probably know about pistol.

Motive.—Gain ? (slight) *Love or Hate ?* Possible with one of his temperament. *Fear ?*
Unlikely.

Note.—Find out who held mortgage. Find out
position of Vyse's firm.

J. ?.—There *could* be a J., *e.g.* an outsider. *But*
with a link in the form of one of the fore-
going. If so, probably connected with A. D.
and E. or F. The existence of J. would explain (1) Ellen's lack of surprise at crime and
her pleasurable satisfaction. (But that might

be due to natural pleasurable excitement of her class over deaths.) (2) The reason for Croft and his wife coming to live in lodge. (3) Might supply motive for F. R.'s *fear* of secret being revealed or for *jealousy*.

Poirot watched me as I read.

" It is very English, is it not ? " he remarked, with pride. " I am more English when I write than when I speak."

" It's an excellent piece of work," I said, warmly. " It sets all the possibilities out most clearly."

" Yes," he said, thoughtfully, as he took it back from me. " And one name leaps to the eye, my friend. *Charles Vyse*. He has the best opportunities. We have given him the choice of two motives. *Ma foi*—if that was a list of racehorses, he would start favourite, *n'est ce pas ?* "

" He is certainly the most likely suspect."

" You have a tendency, Hastings, to prefer the least likely. That, no doubt, is from reading too many detective stories. In real life, nine times out of ten, it is the most likely and the most obvious person who commits the crime."

" But you don't really think that is so this time ? "

" There is only one thing that is against it. The boldness of the crime ! That has stood out from the first. Because of that, as I say, the motive *cannot be obvious*."

" Yes, that is what you said at first."

" And that is what I say again."

With a sudden brusque gesture he crumpled the sheets of paper and threw them on the floor.

"No," he said, as I uttered an exclamation of protest. "That list has been in vain. Still, it has cleared my mind. *Order and method!* That is the first stage. To arrange the facts with neatness and precision. The next stage——"

"Yes."

"The next stage is that of the psychology. The correct employment of the little grey cells ! I advise you, Hastings, to go to bed."

"No," I said. "Not unless you do. I'm not going to leave you."

"Most faithful of dogs ! But see you, Hastings, you cannot assist me to think. That is all I am going to do—think."

I still shook my head.

"You might want to discuss some point with me."

"Well—well—you are a loyal friend. Take at least, I beg of you, the easy-chair."

That proposal I did accept. Presently the room began to swim and dip. The last thing I remember was seeing Poirot carefully retrieving the crumpled sheets of paper from the floor and putting them away tidily in the waste-paper basket.

Then I must have fallen asleep.

CHAPTER X

NICK'S SECRET

It was daylight when I awoke.

Poirot was still sitting where he had been the night before. His attitude was the same, but in his face was a difference. His eyes were shining with that queer cat-like green light that I knew so well.

I struggled to an upright position, feeling very stiff and uncomfortable. Sleeping in a chair is a proceeding not to be recommended at my time of life. Yet one thing at least resulted from it—I awoke not in that pleasant state of lazy somnolence but with a mind and brain as active as when I fell asleep.

"Poirot," I cried. "You have thought of something."

He nodded. He leaned forward, tapping the table in front of him.

"Tell me, Hastings, the answer to these three questions. *Why has Mademoiselle Nick been sleeping badly lately? Why did she buy a black evening dress —she never wears black? Why did she say last night, 'I have nothing to live for—now'?*"

I stared. The questions seemed beside the point.

"Answer those questions, Hastings, answer them?"

"Well—as to the first—she said she had been worried lately."

" Precisely. What has she been worried about ? "

" And the black dress—well, everybody wants a change sometimes."

" For a married man, you have very little appreciation of feminine psychology. If a woman thinks she does not look well in a colour, she refuses to wear it."

" And the last—well, it was a natural thing to say after that awful shock."

" No, *mon ami*, it was *not* a natural thing to say. To be horror-struck by her cousin's death, to reproach herself for it—yes, all that is natural enough. But the other, no. She spoke of life with weariness— as of a thing no longer dear to her. Never before had she displayed that attitude. She had been defiant— yes—she had snapped the fingers, yes—and then, when that broke down, she was afraid. Afraid, mark you, because life was sweet and she did not wish to die. But weary of life—no ! That never ! Even before dinner that was not so. We have there, Hastings, a *psychological change*. And that is interesting. What was it caused her point of view to change ? "

" The shock of her cousin's death."

" I wonder. It was the shock that loosed her tongue. But suppose the change was before that. Is there anything else could account for it ? "

" I don't know of anything."

" Think, Hastings. Use your little grey cells."

" Really——"

" What was the last moment we had the opportunity of observing her ? "

" Well, actually, I suppose, at dinner."

" Exactly. After that, we only saw her receiving guests, making them welcome—purely a formal attitude. What happened at the end of dinner, Hastings ? "

" She went to telephone," I said, slowly.

" *À la bonheur.* You have got there at last. She went to telephone. And she was absent a long time. Twenty minutes at least. That is a long time for a telephone call. Who spoke to her over the telephone? What did they say ? Did she really telephone ? We have got to find out, Hastings, what happened in that twenty minutes. For there, or so I fully believe, we shall find the clue we seek."

" You really think so ? "

" *Mais oui, mais oui !* All along, Hastings, I have told you that Mademoiselle has been keeping something back. She doesn't think it has any connection with the murder—but I, Hercule Poirot, know better ! It *must* have a connection. For all along, I have been conscious that there is a factor lacking. If there were not a factor lacking—why then, the whole thing would be plain to me ! And as it is not plain to me—*eh bien*—then the missing factor is the keystone of the mystery ! I know I am right, Hastings.

" I must know the answer to those three questions. And then—and then—I shall begin *to see.* . . ."

" Well," I said, stretching my stiffened limbs, " I think a bath and a shave are indicated."

By the time I had had a bath and changed into day clothing I felt better. The stiffness and weariness of a night passed in uncomfortable conditions passed off. I arrived at the breakfast table feeling that one drink of hot coffee would restore me to my normal self.

I glanced at the paper, but there was little news in it beyond the fact that Michael Seton's death was now definitely confirmed. The intrepid airman had perished. I wondered whether, to-morrow, new headlines would have sprung into being : " GIRL MURDERED DURING FIREWORK PARTY. MYSTERIOUS TRAGEDY." Something like that.

I had just finished breakfast when Frederica Rice came up to my table. She was wearing a plain little frock of black marocain with a little soft pleated white collar. Her fairness was more evident than ever.

" I want to see M. Poirot, Captain Hastings. Is he up yet, do you know ? "

" I will take you up with me now," I said. " We shall find him in the sitting-room."

" Thank you."

" I hope," I said, as we left the dining-room together, " that you didn't sleep too badly ? "

" It was a shock," she said, in a meditative voice. " But, of course, I didn't know the poor girl. It's not as though it had been Nick."

" I suppose you'd never met this girl before ? "

" Once—at Scarborough. She came over to lunch with Nick."

" It will be a terrible blow to her father and mother," I said.

" Dreadful."

But she said it very impersonally. She was, I fancied, an egoist. Nothing was very real to her that did not concern herself.

Poirot had finished his breakfast and was sitting reading the morning paper. He rose and greeted Frederica with all his customary Gallic politeness.

" Madame," he said. " *Enchanté !* "

He drew forward a chair.

She thanked him with a very faint smile and sat down. Her two hands rested on the arms of the chair. She sat there very upright, looking straight in front of her. She did not rush into speech. There was something a little frightening about her stillness and aloofness.

" M. Poirot," she said at last. " I suppose there is no doubt that this—sad business last night was all part and parcel of the same thing ? I mean—that the intended victim was really Nick ? "

" I should say, Madame, that there was no doubt at all."

Frederica frowned a little.

" Nick bears a charmed life," she said.

There was some curious undercurrent in her voice that I could not understand.

" Luck, they say, goes in cycles," remarked Poirot.

" Perhaps. It is certainly useless to fight against it."

Now there was only weariness in her tone. After a moment or two, she went on.

" I must beg your pardon, M. Poirot. Nick's pardon, too. Up till last night I did not believe. I never dreamed that the danger was—serious."

" Is that so, Madame ? "

" I see now that everything will have to be gone into—carefully. And I imagine that Nick's immediate circle of friends will not be immune from suspicion. Ridiculous, of course, but there it is. Am I right, M. Poirot ? "

" You are very intelligent, Madame."

" You asked me some questions about Tavistock the other day, M. Poirot. As you will find out sooner or later, I might as well tell you the truth now. I was not at Tavistock."

" No, Madame ? "

" I motored down to this part of the world with Mr. Lazarus early last week. We did not wish to arouse more comment than necessary. We stayed at a little place called Shellacombe."

" That is, I think, about seven miles from here, Madame ? "

" About that—yes."

Still that quiet far-away weariness.

" May I be impertinent, Madame ? "

" Is there such a thing—in these days ? "

" Perhaps you are right, Madame. How long have you and M. Lazarus been friends ? "

" I met him six months ago."

" And you—care for him, Madame ? "

Frederica shrugged her shoulders.

" He is—rich."

" Oh ! *là là*," cried Poirot. " That is an ugly thing to say."

She seemed faintly amused.

" Isn't it better to say it myself—than to have you say it for me ? "

" Well—there is always that, of course. May I repeat, Madame, that you are *very* intelligent."

" You will give me a diploma soon," said Frederica, and rose.

" There is nothing more you wish to tell me, Madame ? "

" I do not think so—no. I am going to take some flowers round to Nick and see how she is."

" Ah, that is very *aimable* of you. Thank you, Madame, for your frankness."

She glanced at him sharply, seemed about to speak, then thought better of it and went out of the room, smiling faintly at me as I held the door open for her.

" She is intelligent," said Poirot. " Yes, but so is Hercule Poirot ! "

" What do you mean ? "

" That it is all very well and very pretty to force the richness of M. Lazarus down my throat——"

" I must say that rather disgusted me."

" *Mon cher*, always you have the right reaction in the wrong place. It is not, for the moment, a question of good taste or otherwise. If Madame Rice has a devoted friend who is rich and can give her all she needs—why then obviously Madame Rice would not need to murder her dearest friend for a mere pittance."

" Oh ! " I said.

" *Précisément !* ' Oh ! ' "

" Why didn't you stop her going to the nursing home ? "

" Why should I show my hand ? Is it Hercule Poirot who prevents Mademoiselle Nick from seeing her friends ? *Quelle idée !* It is the doctors and the nurses. Those tiresome nurses ! So full of rules and regulations and ' doctor's orders.' "

" You're not afraid that they may let her in after all ? Nick might insist."

" Nobody will be let in, my dear Hastings, but you and me. And for that matter, the sooner we make our way there, the better."

The sitting-room door flew open and George Challenger barged in. His tanned face was alive with indignation.

" Look here, M. Poirot," he said. " What's the meaning of this ? I rang up that damned nursing home where Nick is. Asked how she was and what time I could come round and see her. And they say the doctor won't allow any visitors. I want to know the meaning of that ? To put it plainly, is this your work ? Or is Nick really ill from shock ? "

" I assure you, Monsieur, that I do not lay down rules for nursing homes. I would not dare. Why not ring up the good doctor—what was his name now ? —Ah, yes, Graham."

" I have. He says she's going on as well as could be expected—usual stuff. But I know all the tricks— my uncle's a doctor. Harley Street. Nerve specialist. Psycho-analysis—all the rest of it. Putting relations and friends off with soothing words. I've heard about it all. I don't believe Nick isn't up to seeing any one. I believe you're at the bottom of this, M. Poirot."

Poirot smiled at him in a very kindly fashion.

Indeed, I have always observed that Poirot has a kindly feeling for a lover.

"Now listen to me, *mon ami*," he said. "If one guest is admitted, others cannot be kept out. You comprehend? It must be all or none. We want Mademoiselle's safety, you and I, do we not? Exactly. Then, you understand—it must be *none*."

"I get you," said Challenger, slowly. "But then——"

"Chut! We will say no more. We will forget even what we have said. The prudence, the extreme prudence, is what is needed at present."

"I can hold my tongue," said the sailor quietly.

He turned away to the door, pausing as he went out to say:

"No embargo on flowers, is there? So long as they are not white ones."

Poirot smiled.

"And now," he said, as the door shut behind the impetuous Challenger, "whilst M. Challenger and Madame and perhaps M. Lazarus all encounter each other in the flower shop, you and I will drive quietly to our destination."

"And ask for the answer to the three questions?" I said.

"Yes. We will ask. Though, as a matter of fact, I know the answer."

"What?" I exclaimed.

"Yes."

"But when did you find out?"

"Whilst I was eating my breakfast, Hastings. It stared me in the face."

" Tell me."

" No, I will leave you to hear it from Mademoiselle."

Then, as if to distract my mind, he pushed an open letter across to me.

It was a report by the expert Poirot had sent to examine the picture of old Nicholas Buckley. It stated definitely that the picture was worth at most twenty pounds.

" So that is one matter cleared up," said Poirot.

" No mouse in that mousehole," I said, remembering a metaphor of Poirot's on one past occasion.

" Ah ! you remember that ? No, as you say, no mouse in that mousehole. Twenty pounds and M. Lazarus offered fifty. What an error of judgment for a seemingly astute young man. But there, there, we must start on our errand."

The nursing home was set high on a hill overlooking the bay. A white-coated orderly received us. We were put into a little room downstairs and presently a brisk-looking nurse came to us.

One glance at Poirot seemed to be enough. She had clearly received her instructions from Dr. Graham together with a minute description of the little detective. She even concealed a smile.

" Miss Buckley has passed a very fair night," she said. " Come up, will you ? "

In a pleasant room with the sun streaming into it, we found Nick. In the narrow iron bed, she looked like a tired child. Her face was white and her eyes were suspiciously red, and she seemed listless and weary.

" It's good of you to come," she said in a flat voice.

Poirot took her hand in both of his.

" Courage, Mademoiselle. There is always something to live for."

The words startled her. She looked up in his face.

" Oh ! " she said. " Oh ! "

" Will you not tell me now, Mademoiselle, what it was that has been worrying you lately ? Or shall I guess ? And may I offer you, Mademoiselle, my very deepest sympathy."

Her face flushed.

" So you know. Oh, well, it doesn't matter who knows now. Now that it's all over. Now that I shall never see him again."

Her voice broke.

" Courage, Mademoiselle."

" I haven't got any courage left. I've used up every bit in these last weeks. Hoping and hoping and —just lately—hoping against hope."

I stared. I could not understand one word.

" Regard the poor Hastings," said Poirot. " He does not know what we are talking about."

Her unhappy eyes met mine.

" Michael Seton, the airman," she said. " I was engaged to him—and he's dead."

CHAPTER XI

THE MOTIVE

I WAS dumfounded.

I turned on Poirot.

" Is this what you meant ? "

" Yes, *mon ami*. This morning—I knew."

" How did you know ? How did you guess ?. You said it stared you in the face at breakfast."

" So it did, my friend. From the front page of the newspaper. I remembered the conversation at dinner last night—and I saw everything."

He turned to Nick again.

" You heard the news last night ? "

" Yes. On the wireless. I made an excuse about the telephone. I wanted to hear the news alone— in case. . . ." She swallowed hard. " And I heard it. . . ."

" I know. I know." He took her hand in both of his.

" It was—pretty ghastly. And all the people arriving. I don't know how I got through it. It all felt like a dream. I could see myself from outside —behaving just as usual. It was queer somehow."

" Yes, yes, I understand."

" And then, when I went to fetch Freddie's wrap— I broke down for a minute. I pulled myself together

129   I

quite quickly. But Maggie kept calling up about her coat. And then at last she took my shawl and went, and I put on some powder and some rouge and followed her out. And there she was—dead. . . ."

" Yes, yes, it must have been a terrible shock."

" You don't understand. I was angry ! I wished it had been *me* ! I wanted to be dead—and there I was —alive and perhaps to live for years ! And Michael dead—drowned far away in the Pacific."

" *Pauvre enfant.*"

" I don't want to be alive. I don't want to live, I tell you ! " she cried, rebelliously.

" I know—I know. To all of us, Mademoiselle, there comes a time when death is preferable to life. But it passes—sorrow passes and grief. You cannot believe that now, I know. It is useless for an old man like me to talk. Idle words—that is what you think—idle words."

" You think I'll forget—and marry someone else? Never ! "

She looked rather lovely as she sat up in bed, her two hands clenched and her cheeks burning.

Poirot said gently :

" No, no. I am not thinking anything of the kind. You are very lucky, Mademoiselle. You have been loved by a brave man—a hero. How did you come to meet him ? "

" It was at Le Touquet—last September. Nearly a year ago."

" And you became engaged—when ? "

" Just after Christmas. But it had to be a secret."

" Why was that ? "

" Michael's uncle—old Sir Matthew Seton. He loved birds and hated women."

" *Ah ! ce n'est pas raisonable !* "

" Well—I don't mean quite that. He was a complete crank. Thought women ruined a man's life. And Michael was absolutely dependent on him. He was frightfully proud of Michael and it was he who financed the building of the *Albatross* and the expenses of the round-the-world flight. It was the dearest dream of his life as well as of Michael's. If Michael had pulled it off—well, then he could have asked his uncle anything. And even if old Sir Matthew had still cut up rough, well, it wouldn't have really mattered. Michael would have been made —a kind of world hero. His uncle would have come round in the end."

" Yes, yes, I see."

" But Michael said it would be fatal if anything leaked out. We must keep it a dead secret. And I did. I never told anyone—not even Freddie."

Poirot groaned.

" If only you had told me, Mademoiselle."

Nick stared at him.

" But what difference would it have made ? It couldn't have anything to do with these mysterious attacks on me ? No, I'd promised Michael—and I kept my word. But it was awful—the anxiety, wondering and getting in a state the whole time. And everyone saying one was so nervy. And being unable to explain."

" Yes, I comprehend all that."

" He was missing once before, you know. Crossing

the desert on the way to India. That was pretty awful, and then after all, it was all right. His machine was damaged, but it was put right, and he went on. And I kept saying to myself that it would be the same this time. Everyone said he must be dead—and I kept telling myself that he must be all right, really. And then—last night. . . ."

Her voice trailed away.

" You had hoped up till then ? "

" I don't know. I think it was more that I refused to believe. It was awful never being able to talk to anyone."

" Yes, I can imagine that. Were you never tempted to tell Madame Rice, for instance ? "

" Sometimes I wanted to frightfully."

" You do not think she—guessed ? "

" I don't think so." Nick considered the idea carefully. " She never said anything. Of course she used to hint things sometimes. About our being great friends and all that."

" You never considered telling her when M. Seton's uncle died ? You know that he died about a week ago ? "

" I know. He had an operation or something. I suppose I might have told anybody then. But it wouldn't have been a nice way of doing it, would it ? I mean, it would have seemed rather boastful—to do it just then—when all the papers were full of Michael. And reporters would have come and interviewed me. It would all have been rather cheap. And Michael would have hated it."

" I agree with you, Mademoiselle. You could not

have announced it publicly. I only meant that you could have spoken of it privately to a friend."

" I did sort of hint to one person," said Nick. " I—thought it was only fair. But I don't know how much he—the person took in."

Poirot nodded.

" Are you on good terms with your cousin, M. Vyse ? " he asked, with a rather abrupt change of subject.

" Charles ? What put him into your head ? "

" I was just wondering—that was all."

" Charles means well," said Nick. " He's a frightful stick, of course. Never moves out of this place. He disapproves of me, I think."

" Oh ! Mademoiselle, Mademoiselle. And I hear that he has laid all his devotion at your feet ! "

" Disapproving of a person doesn't keep you from having a pash for them. Charles thinks my mode of life is reprehensible and he disapproves of my cocktails, my complexion, my friends and my conversation. But he still feels my fatal fascination. He always hopes to reform me, I think."

She paused and then said, with a ghost of a twinkle :

" Who have you been pumping to get the local information ? "

" You must not give me away, Mademoiselle. I had a little conversation with the Australian lady, Madame Croft."

" She's rather an old dear—when one has time for her. Terribly sentimental. Love and home and children—you know the sort of thing."

"I am old-fashioned and sentimental myself, Mademoiselle."

"Are you? I should have said that Captain Hastings was the sentimental one of you two."

I blushed indignantly.

"He is furious," said Poirot, eyeing my discomfiture with a good deal of pleasure. "But you are right, Mademoiselle. Yes, you are right."

"Not at all," I said, angrily.

"Hastings has a singularly beautiful nature. It has been the greatest hindrance to me at times."

"Don't be absurd, Poirot."

"He is, to begin with, reluctant to see evil anywhere, and when he does see it his righteous indignation is so great that he is incapable of dissembling. Altogether a rare and beautiful nature. No, *mon ami*, I will not permit you to contradict me. It is as I say."

"You've both been very kind to me," said Nick, gently.

"*Là, là*, Mademoiselle. That is nothing. We have much more to do. To begin with, you will remain here. You will obey orders. You will do what I tell you. At this juncture I must not be hampered."

Nick sighed wearily.

"I'll do anything you like. I don't care what I do."

"You will see no friends for the present."

"I don't care. I don't want to see anyone."

"For you the passive part—for us the active one. Now, Mademoiselle, I am going to leave you. I will not intrude longer upon your sorrow."

He moved towards the door, pausing with his hand on the handle to say over his shoulder :

" By the way, you once mentioned a will you made. Where is it, this will ? "

" Oh ! it's knocking round somewhere."

" At End House ? "

" Yes."

" In a safe ? Locked up in your desk ? "

" Well, I really don't know. It's somewhere about." She frowned. " I'm frightfully untidy, you know. Papers and things like that would be mostly in the writing-table in the library. That's where most of the bills are. The will is probably with them. Or it might be in my bedroom."

" You permit me to make the search—yes ? "

" If you want to—yes. Look at anything you like."

" *Merci*, Mademoiselle. I will avail myself of your permission."

CHAPTER XII

ELLEN

POIROT said no word till we had emerged from the nursing home into the outer air. Then he caught me by the arm.

"You see, Hastings? You see? Ah! *Sacré tonnerre!* I was right! I was right! Always I knew there was something lacking—some piece of the puzzle that was not there. And without that missing piece the whole thing was meaningless."

His almost despairing triumph was double-Dutch to me. I could not see that anything very epoch-making had occurred.

"It was there all the time. And I could not see it. But how should I? To know there is *something*—that, yes—but to know what that something is. *Ah! Ca c'est bien plus difficile.*"

"Do you mean that this has some direct bearing on the crime?"

"*Ma foi*, do you not see?"

"As a matter of fact, I don't."

"Is it possible? Why, it gives us what we have been looking for—the motive—the hidden obscure motive!"

"I may be very dense, but I can't see it. Do you mean jealousy of some kind?"

" Jealousy ? No, no, my friend. The usual motive —the inevitable motive. Money, my friend, money!"

I stared. He went on, speaking more calmly.

" Listen, *mon ami*. Just over a week ago Sir Matthew Seton dies. And Sir Matthew Seton was a millionaire—one of the richest men in England."

" Yes, but——"

" *Attendez*. One step at a time. He has a nephew whom he idolises and to whom, we may safely assume, he has left his vast fortune."

" But——"

" *Mais oui*—legacies, yes, an endowment to do with his hobby, yes, but the bulk of the money would go to Michael Seton. Last Tuesday, Michael Seton is reported missing—*and on Wednesday the attacks on Mademoiselle's life begin.* Supposing, Hastings, that Michael Seton made a will before he started on this flight, and that in that will he left all he had to his fiancée."

" That's pure supposition."

" It is supposition—yes. *But it must be so.* Because, if it is not so, there is no meaning in anything that has happened. It is no paltry inheritance that is at stake. It is an enormous fortune."

I was silent for some minutes, turning the matter over in my mind. It seemed to me that Poirot was leaping at conclusions in a most reckless manner, and yet I was secretly convinced that he was right. It was his extraordinary flair for being right that influenced me. Yet it seemed to me that there was a good deal to be proved still.

"But if nobody knew of the engagement," I argued.

" Pah ! Somebody *did* know. For the matter of that, somebody always *does* know. If they do not know, they guess. Madame Rice suspected. Mademoiselle Nick admitted as much. She may have had means of turning those suspicions into certainties."

" How ? "

" Well, for one thing, there must have been letters from Michael Seton to Mademoiselle Nick. They had been engaged some time. And her best friend could not call that young lady anything but careless. She leaves things here and there, and everywhere. I doubt if she has ever locked up anything in her life. Oh, yes, there would be means of making sure."

" And Frederica Rice would know about the will that her friend had made ? "

" Doubtless. Oh, yes, it narrows down now. You remember my list—a list of persons numbered from A. to J. It has narrowed down to only two persons. I dismiss the servants. I dismiss the Commander Challenger—even though he did take one hour and a half to reach here from Plymouth—and the distance is only thirty miles. I dismiss the long-nosed M. Lazarus who offered fifty pounds for a picture that was only worth twenty (it is odd, that, when you come to think of it. Most uncharacteristic of his race). I dismiss the Australians—so hearty and so pleasant. I keep two people on my list still."

" One is Frederica Rice," I said, slowly.

I had a vision of her face, the golden hair, the white fragility of the features.

" Yes. She is indicated very clearly. However

carelessly worded Mademoiselle's will may have been, she would be plainly indicated as residuary legatee. Apart from End House, everything was to go to her. If Mademoiselle Nick instead of Mademoiselle Maggie had been shot last night, Madame Rice would be a rich woman to-day."

" I can hardly believe it ! "

" You mean that you can hardly believe that a beautiful woman can be a murderess ? One often has a little difficulty with members of a jury on that account. But you may be right. There is still another suspect."

" Who ? "

" Charles Vyse."

" But he only inherits the house."

" Yes—but he may not know that. Did he make Mademoiselle's will for her ? I think not. If so, it would be in his keeping, not " knocking around somewhere," or whatever the phrase was that Mademoiselle used. So, you see, Hastings, *it is quite probable that he knows nothing about that will.* He may believe that she has never made a will and that, in that case, he will inherit as next of kin."

" You know," I said, " that really seems to me much more probable."

" That is your romantic mind, Hastings. The wicked solicitor. A familiar figure in fiction. If as well as being a solicitor he has an impassive face, it makes the matter almost certain. It is true that, in some ways, he is more in the picture than Madame. He would be more likely to know about the pistol and more likely to use one."

" And to send the boulder crashing down."

" Perhaps. Though, as I have told you, much can be done by leverage. And the fact that the boulder was dislodged at the wrong minute, and consequently missed Mademoiselle, is more suggestive of feminine agency. The idea of tampering with the interior of a car seems masculine in conception—though many women are as good mechanics as men nowadays. On the other hand, there are one or two gaps in the theory against M. Vyse."

" Such as—— ? "

" He is less likely to have known of the engagement than Madame. And there is another point. His action was rather precipitate."

" What do you mean ? "

" Well, until last night there was no *certitude* that Seton was dead. To act rashly, without due assurance, seems very uncharacteristic of the legal mind."

" Yes," I said. " A woman would jump to conclusions."

" Exactly. *Ce que femme veut, Dieu veut.* That is the attitude."

" It's really amazing the way Nick has escaped. It seems almost incredible."

And suddenly I remembered the tone in Frederica's voice as she had said : " Nick bears a charmed life."

I shivered a little.

" Yes," said Poirot, thoughtfully. " And I can take no credit to myself. Which is humiliating."

" Providence," I murmured.

" Ah ! *mon ami*, I would not put on the shoulders of the good God the burden of men's wrongdoing.

You say that in your Sunday morning voice of thankfulness—without reflecting that what you are really saying is that *le bon Dieu* has killed Miss Maggie Buckley."

" Really, Poirot ! "

" Really, my friend ! But I will not sit back and say ' *le bon Dieu* has arranged everything, I will not interfere.' Because I am convinced that *le bon Dieu* created Hercule Poirot for the express purpose of interfering. It is my *métier*."

We had been slowly ascending the zig-zag path up the cliff. It was at this juncture that we passed through the little gate into the grounds of End House.

" Pouf ! " said Poirot. " That ascent is a steep one. I am hot. My moustaches are limp. Yes, as I was saying just now, I am on the side of the innocent. I am on the side of Mademoiselle Nick because she was attacked. I am on the side of Mademoiselle Maggie because she has been killed."

" And you are against Frederica Rice and Charles Vyse."

" No, no, Hastings. I keep an open mind. I say only that at the moment one of those two is indicated. Chut ! "

We had come out on the strip of lawn by the house, and a man was driving a mowing machine. He had a long, stupid face and lack-lustre eyes. Beside him was a small boy of about ten, ugly but intelligent-looking.

It crossed my mind that we had not heard the mowing machine in action, but I presumed that the gardener was not overworking himself. He had probably been resting from his labours, and had sprung into action on hearing our voices approaching.

" Good-morning," said Poirot.

" Good-morning, sir."

" You are the gardener, I suppose. The husband of Madame who works in the house."

" He's my Dad," said the small boy.

" That's right, sir," said the man. " You'll be the foreign gentleman, I take it, that's really a detective. Is there any news of the young mistress, sir ? "

" I come from seeing her at the immediate moment. She has passed a satisfactory night."

" We've had policemen here," said the small boy. " That's where the lady was killed. Here by the steps. I seen a pig killed once, haven't I, Dad ? "

" Ah ! " said his father, unemotionally.

" Dad used to kill pigs when he worked on a farm. Didn't you, Dad ? I seen a pig killed. I liked it."

" Young 'uns like to see pigs killed," said the man, as though stating one of the unalterable facts of nature.

" Shot with a pistol, the lady was," continued the boy. " She didn't have her throat cut. No ! "

We passed on to the house, and I felt thankful to get away from the ghoulish child.

Poirot entered the drawing-room, the windows of which were open and rang the bell. Ellen, neatly attired in black, came in answer to the bell. She showed no surprise at seeing us.

Poirot explained that we were here by permission of Miss Buckley to make a search of the house.

" Very good, sir."

" The police have finished ? "

" They said they had seen everything they wanted, sir. They've been about the garden since very early in the morning. I don't know whether they've found anything."

She was about to leave the room when Poirot stopped her with a question.

" Were you very surprised last night when you heard Miss Buckley had been shot ? "

" Yes, sir, very surprised. Miss Maggie was a nice young lady, sir. I can't imagine anyone being so wicked as to want to harm her."

" If it had been anyone else, you would not have been so surprised—eh ? "

" I don't know what you mean, sir ? "

" When I came into the hall last night," I said, " you asked at once whether anyone had been hurt. Were you expecting anything of the kind ? "

She was silent. Her fingers pleated a corner of her apron. She shook her head and murmured :

" You gentlemen wouldn't understand."

" Yes, yes," said Poirot, " I would understand. However fantastic what you may say, I would understand."

She looked at him doubtfully, then seemed to make up her mind to trust him.

" You see, sir," she said, " this isn't a good house."

I was surprised and a little contemptuous. Poirot, however, seemed to find the remark not in the least unusual.

" You mean it is an old house."

" Yes, sir, not a good house."

" You have been here long ? "

" Six years, sir. But I was here as a girl. In the kitchen as kitchen-maid. That was in the time of old Sir Nicholas. It was the same then."

Poirot looked at her attentively

" In an old house," he said, " there is sometimes an atmosphere of evil."

" That's it, sir," said Ellen, eagerly. " Evil. Bad thoughts and bad deeds too. It's like dry rot in a house, sir, you can't get it out. It's a sort of feeling in the air. I always knew something bad would happen in this house, some day."

" Well, you have been proved right."

" Yes, sir."

There was a very slight underlying satisfaction in her tone, the satisfaction of one whose gloomy prognostications have been shown to be correct.

" But you didn't think it would be Miss Maggie."

" No, indeed, I didn't, sir. Nobody hated *her*— I'm sure of it."

It seemed to me that in those words was a clue. I expected Poirot to follow it up, but to my surprise he shifted to quite a different subject.

" You didn't hear the shots fired ? "

" I couldn't have told with the fireworks going on. Very noisy they were."

" You weren't out watching them ? "

" No, I hadn't finished clearing up dinner."

" Was the waiter helping you ? "

" No, sir, he'd gone out into the garden to have a look at the fireworks."

" But you didn't go."

" No, sir."

" Why was that ? "

" I wanted to get finished."

" You don't care for fireworks ? "

" Oh, yes, sir, it wasn't that. But you see, there's two nights of them, and William and I get the evening off to-morrow and go down into the town and see them from there."

" I comprehend. And you heard Mademoiselle Maggie asking for her coat and unable to find it ? "

" I heard Miss Nick run upstairs, sir, and Miss Buckley call up from the front hall saying she couldn't find something and I heard her say, ' All right—I'll take the shawl——' "

" Pardon," Poirot interrupted. " You did not endeavour to search for the coat for her—or get it from the car where it had been left."

" I had my work to do, sir."

" Quite so—and doubtless neither of the two young ladies asked you because they thought you were out looking at the fireworks ? "

" Yes, sir."

" So that, other years, you *have* been out looking at the fireworks ? "

A sudden flush came into her pale cheek.

" I don't know what you mean, sir. We're always allowed to go out into the garden. If I didn't feel like it this year, and would rather get on with my work and go to bed, well, that's my business, I imagine."

" *Mais oui. Mais oui.* I did not intend to offend

K

you. Why should you not do as you prefer. To make
a change, it is pleasant."

He paused and then added :

" Now another little matter in which I wonder
whether you can help me. This is an old house. Are
there, do you know, any secret chambers in it ? "

" Well—there's a kind of sliding panel—in this
very room. I remember being shown it as a girl.
Only I can't remember just now where it is. Or was
it in the library ? I can't say, I'm sure."

" Big enough for a person to hide in ? "

" Oh, no, indeed, sir ! A little cupboard place—
a kind of niche. About a foot square, sir, not more
than that."

" Oh ! that is not what I mean at all."

The blush rose to her face again.

" If you think I was hiding anywhere—I wasn't !
I heard Miss Nick run down the stairs and out and I
heard her cry out—and I came into the hall to see if
—if anything was the matter. And that's the gospel
truth, sir. That's the gospel truth."

CHAPTER XIII

LETTERS

HAVING successfully got rid of Ellen, Poirot turned a somewhat thoughtful face towards me.

" I wonder now—did she hear those shots ? I think she did. She heard them, she opened the kitchen door. She heard Nick rush down the stairs and out, and she herself came into the hall to find out what had happened. That is natural enough. But why did she not go out and watch the fireworks that evening ? That is what I should like to know, Hastings."

" What was your idea in asking about a secret hiding place ? "

" A mere fanciful idea that, after all, we might not have disposed of J."

" J ? "

" Yes. The last person on my list. The problematical outsider. Supposing for some reason connected with Ellen, that J. had come to the house last night. He (I assume a he) conceals himself in a secret chamber in this room. A girl passes through whom he takes to be Nick. He follows her out—and shoots her. *Non—c'est idiot !* And anyway, we know that there is no hiding place. Ellen's decision to remain in the kitchen last night was a pure hazard. Come, let us search for the will of Mademoiselle Nick."

There were no papers in the drawing-room. We adjourned to the library, a rather dark room looking out on the drive. Here there was a large old-fashioned walnut bureau-writing-table.

It took us some time to go through it. Everything was in complete confusion. Bills and receipts were mixed up together. Letters of invitation, letters pressing for payment of accounts, letters from friends.

"We will arrange these papers," said Poirot, sternly, "with order and method."

He was as good as his word. Half an hour later, he sat back with a pleased expression on his face. Everything was neatly sorted, docketed and filed.

"*C'est bien, ça.* One thing is at least to the good. We have had to go through everything so thoroughly that there is no possibility of our having missed anything."

"No, indeed. Not that there's been much to find."

"Except possibly this."

He tossed across a letter. It was written in large sprawling handwriting, almost indecipherable.

"DARLING,—Party was too too marvellous. Feel rather a worm to-day. You were wise not to touch that stuff—don't ever start, darling. It's too damned hard to give up. I'm writing the boy friend to hurry up the supply. What Hell life is !

"Yours,
"FREDDIE."

"Dated last February," said Poirot, thoughtfully. "She takes drugs, of course, I knew that as soon as I looked at her."

" Really ? I never suspected such a thing."

" It is fairly obvious. You have only to look at her eyes. And then there are her extraordinary variations of mood. Sometimes she is all on edge, strung up—sometimes she is lifeless—inert."

" Drug-taking affects the moral sense, does it not ? "

" Inevitably. But I do not think Madame Rice is a real addict. She is at the beginning—not the end."

" And Nick ? "

" There are no signs of it. She may have attended a dope party now and then for fun, but she is no taker of drugs."

" I'm glad of that."

I remembered suddenly what Nick had said about Frederica that she was not always herself. Poirot nodded and tapped the letter he held.

" This is what she was referring to, undoubtedly. Well, we have drawn the blank, as you say, here. Let us go up to Mademoiselle's room."

There was a desk in Nick's room also, but comparatively little was kept in it. Here again, there was no sign of a will. We found the registration book of her car and a perfectly good dividend warrant of a month back. Otherwise there was nothing of importance.

Poirot sighed in an exasperated fashion.

" The young girls—they are not properly trained nowadays. The order, the method, it is left out of their bringing up. She is charming, Mademoiselle Nick, but she is a feather-head. Decidedly she is a feather-head."

He was now going through the contents of a chest of drawers.

" Surely, Poirot," I said, with some embarrassment, " those are underclothes."

He paused in surprise.

" And why not, my friend ? "

" Don't you think—I mean—we can hardly——"

He broke into a roar of laughter.

" Decidedly, my poor Hastings, you belong to the Victorian era. Mademoiselle Nick would tell you so if she were here. In all probability she would say that you had the mind like the sink ! Young ladies are not ashamed of their underclothes nowadays. The camisole, the cami-knicker, it is no longer a shameful secret. Every day, on the beach, all these garments will be discarded within a few feet of you. And why not ? "

" I don't see any need for what you are doing."

" *Écoutez*, my friend. Clearly, she does not lock up her treasures, Mademoiselle Nick. If she wished to hide anything from sight—where would she hide it ? Underneath the stockings and the petticoats. Ah ! what have we here ? "

He held up a packet of letters tied with a faded pink ribbon.

" The love letters of M. Michael Seton, if I mistake not."

Quite calmly he untied the ribbon and began to open out the letters.

" Poirot," I cried, scandalised. " You really **can't** do that. It isn't playing the game."

" I am not playing a game, *mon ami*." His voice

rang out suddenly harsh and stern. " I am hunting down a murderer."

" Yes, but private letters——"

" May have nothing to tell me—on the other hand, they may. I must take every chance, my friend. Come, you might as well read them with me. Two pairs of eyes are no worse than one pair. Console yourself with the thought that the staunch Ellen probably knows them by heart."

I did not like it. Still I realised that in Poirot's position he could not afford to be squeamish, and I consoled myself by the quibble that Nick's last word had been, " Look at anything you like."

The letters spread over several dates, beginning last winter.

New Year's Day.

" DARLING,—The New Year is in and I'm making good resolutions. It seems too wonderful to be true —that you should actually love me. You've made all the difference to my life. I believe we both knew —from the very first moment we met. Happy New Year, my lovely girl.

" Yours for ever,
" MICHAEL."

February 8th.

" DEAREST LOVE,—How I wish I could see you more often. This is pretty rotten, isn't it ? I hate all this beastly concealment, but I explained to you how things are. I know how much you hate lies and concealment. I do too. But honestly, it might upset the whole apple cart. Uncle Matthew has got an absolute bee in his bonnet about early marriages and the way they wreck a man's career. As though you could wreck mine, you dear angel!

" Cheer up, darling. Everything will come right.

" Yours,
" MICHAEL."

March 2nd.

" I oughtn't to write to you two days running, I know. But I must. When I was up yesterday I thought of you. I flew over Scarborough. Blessed, blessed, blessed Scarborough—the most wonderful place in the world. Darling, you don't know how I love you!

" Yours,
" MICHAEL."

April 18th.

" DEAREST, — The whole thing is fixed up. Definitely. If I pull this off (and I shall pull it off) I shall be able to take a firm line with Uncle Matthew —and if he doesn't like it—well, what do I care? It's adorable of you to be so interested in my long technical descriptions of the *Albatross*. How I long to take you up in her. Some day! Don't for goodness' sake, worry about me. The thing isn't half so risky as it sounds. I simply couldn't get killed now that I know you care for me. Everything will be all right, sweetheart. Trust your Michael."

April 20th.

" YOU ANGEL,—Every word you say is true and I
shall treasure that letter always. I'm not half good
enough for you. You are so different from everybody
else. I adore you.

" Your
" MICHAEL."

The last was undated.

" DEAREST,—Well—I'm off to-morrow. Feeling
tremendously keen and excited and absolutely
certain of success. The old *Albatross* is all tuned up.
She won't let me down.

" Cheer up, sweetheart, and don't worry. There's
a risk, of course, but all life's risk really. By the
way, somebody said I ought to make a will (tactful
fellow—but he meant well), so I have—on a half
sheet of notepaper—and sent it to old Whitfield. I'd
no time to go round there. Somebody once told me
that a man made a will of three words, ' All to
Mother,' and it was legal all right. My will was
rather like that—I remembered your name was
really Magdala, which was clever of me ! A couple
of the fellows witnessed it.

" Don't take all this solemn talk about wills to
heart, will you ? (I didn't mean that pun. An
accident.) I shall be as right as rain. I'll send you
telegrams from India and Australia and so on. And
keep up heart. *It's going to be all right.* See ?

" Good-night and God bless you,

" MICHAEL."

Poirot folded the letters together again.

" You see, Hastings ? I had to read them—to make sure. It is as I told you."

" Surely you could have found out some other way ? "

" No, *mon cher*, that is just what I could not do. It had to be this way. We have now some very valuable evidence."

" In what way ? "

" We now know that the fact of Michael's having made a will in favour of Mademoiselle Nick is actually recorded in writing. Anyone who had read those letters would know the fact. And with letters carelessly hidden like that, anyone could read them."

" Ellen ? "

" Ellen, almost certainly, I should say. We will try a little experiment on her before passing out."

" There is no sign of the will."

" No, that is curious. But in all probability it is thrown on top of a bookcase, or inside a china jar. We must try to awaken Mademoiselle's memory on that point. At any rate, there is nothing more to be found here."

Ellen was dusting the hall as we descended.

Poirot wished her good-morning very pleasantly as we passed. He turned back from the front door to say :

" You knew, I suppose, that Miss Buckley was engaged to the airman, Michael Seton ? "

She stared.

" What ? The one there's all the fuss in the papers about ? "

" Yes."

" Well, I never. To think of that. Engaged to Miss Nick."

" Complete and absolute surprise registered very convincingly," I remarked, as we got outside.

" Yes. It really seemed genuine."

" Perhaps it was," I suggested.

" And that packet of letters reclining for months under the *lingerie*? No, *mon ami*."

" All very well," I thought to myself. " But we are not all Hercule Poirots. We do not all go nosing into what does not concern us."

But I said nothing.

" This Ellen—she is an enigma," said Poirot. " I do not like it. There is something here that I do not understand."

CHAPTER XIV

THE MYSTERY OF THE MISSING WILL

WE went straight back to the nursing home.

Nick looked rather surprised to see us.

" Yes, Mademoiselle," said Poirot, answering her look. " I am like the Jack in the Case. I pop up again. To begin with I will tell you that I have put the order in your affairs. Everything is now neatly. arranged."

" Well, I expect it was about time," said Nick, unable to help smiling. " Are you *very* tidy, M. Poirot ? "

" Ask my friend Hastings here."

The girl turned an inquiring gaze on me.

I detailed some of Poirot's minor peculiarities— toast that had to be made from a square loaf—eggs matching in size—his objection to golf as a game " shapeless and haphazard," whose only redeeming feature was the tee boxes ! I ended by telling her the famous case which Poirot had solved by his habit of straightening ornaments on the mantelpiece.

Poirot sat by smiling.

" He makes the good tale of it, yes," he said, when I had finished. " But on the whole it is true. Figure to yourself, Mademoiselle, that I never cease trying to persuade Hastings to part his hair in the middle instead of on the side. See what an air, lop-sided and unsymmetrical, it gives him."

"Then you must disapprove of me, M. Poirot," said Nick. "I wear a side parting. And you must approve of Freddie who parts her hair in the middle."

"He was certainly admiring her the other evening," I put in maliciously. "Now I know the reason."

"*C'est assez*," said Poirot. "I am here on serious business. Mademoiselle, this will of yours, I find it not."

"Oh!" She wrinkled her brows. "But does it matter so much? After all, I'm not dead. And wills aren't really important till you are dead, are they?"

"That is correct. All the same, I interest myself in this will of yours. I have various little ideas concerning it. Think, Mademoiselle. Try to remember where you placed it—where you saw it last?"

"I don't suppose I put it anywhere particular," said Nick. "I never do put things in places. I probably shoved it into a drawer."

"You did not put it in the secret panel by any chance?"

"The secret *what*?"

"Your maid, Ellen, says that there is a secret panel in the drawing-room or the library."

"Nonsense," said Nick. "I've never heard of such a thing. *Ellen* said so?"

"*Mais oui*. It seems she was in service at End House as a young girl. The cook showed it to her."

"It's the first I've ever heard of it. I suppose Grandfather must have known about it, but, if so, he didn't tell me. And I'm sure he *would* have told me. M. Poirot, are you sure Ellen isn't making it all up ? "

" No, Mademoiselle, I am not at all sure ! *Il me semble* that there is something—odd about this Ellen of yours."

" Oh ! I wouldn't call her odd. William's a half-wit, and the child is a nasty little brute, but Ellen's all right. The essence of respectability."

" Did you give her leave to go out and see the fireworks last night, Mademoiselle ? "

" Of course. They always do. They clear up afterwards."

" Yet she did not go out."

" Oh, yes, she did."

" How do you know, Mademoiselle ? "

" Well—well—I suppose I don't know. I told her to go and she thanked me—and so, of course, I assumed that she did go."

" On the contrary—she remained in the house."

" But—how very odd ! "

" You think it odd ? "

" Yes, I do. I'm sure she's never done such a thing before. Did she say why ? "

" She did not tell me the real reason—of that I am sure."

Nick looked at him questioningly.

" Is it—important ? "

Poirot flung out his hands.

" That is just what I cannot say, Mademoiselle. *C'est curieux.* I leave it like that."

" This panel business too," said Nick, reflectively. " I can't help thinking that's frightfully queer—and unconvincing. Did she show you where it was?"

"She said she couldn't remember."

"I don't believe there is such a thing."

"It certainly looks like it."

"She must be going batty, poor thing."

"She certainly recounts the histories! She said also that End House was not a good house to live in."

Nick gave a little shiver.

"Perhaps she's right there," she said slowly. "Sometimes I've felt that way myself. There's a queer feeling in that house. . . ."

Her eyes grew large and dark. They had a fated look. Poirot hastened to recall her to other topics.

"We have wandered from our subject, Mademoiselle. The will. The last will and testament of Magdala Buckley."

"I put that," said Nick, with some pride. "I remember putting that, and I said pay all debts and testamentary expenses. I remembered that out of a book I'd read."

"You did not use a will form, then?"

"No, there wasn't time for that. I was just going off to the nursing home, and besides Mr. Croft said will forms were very dangerous. It was better to make a simple will and not try to be too legal."

"M. Croft? He was there?"

"Yes. It was he who asked me if I'd made one. I'd never have thought of it myself. He said if you died in—in——"

"Intestate," I said.

"Yes, that's it. He said if you died intestate, the Crown pinched a lot and that would be a pity."

" Very helpful, the excellent M. Croft ! "

" Oh, he was," said Nick warmly. " He got Ellen in and her husband to witness it. Oh ! of course ! What an idiot I've been ! "

We looked at her inquiringly.

" I've been a perfect idiot. Letting you hunt round End House. Charles has got it, of course ! My cousin, Charles Vyse."

" Ah ! so that is the explanation."

" Mr. Croft said a lawyer was the proper person to have charge of it."

" *Trés correcte, ce bon M. Croft.*"

" Men are useful sometimes," said Nick. " A lawyer or the Bank—that's what he said. And I said Charles would be best. So we stuck it in an envelope and sent it off to him straight away."

She lay back on her pillows with a sigh.

" I'm sorry I've been so frightfully stupid. But it is all right now. Charles has got it, and if you really want to see it, of course he'll show it to you."

" Not without an authorisation from you," said Poirot, smiling.

" How silly."

" No, Mademoiselle. Merely prudent."

" Well, I think it's silly." She took a piece of paper from a little stack that lay beside her bed. " What shall I say ? Let the dog see the rabbit ? "

" *Comment ?* "

I laughed at his startled face.

He dictated a form of words, and Nick wrote obediently.

" Thank you, Mademoiselle," said Poirot, as he took it.

" I'm sorry to have given you such a lot of trouble. But I really had forgotten. You know how one forgets things almost at once ? "

" With order and method in the mind one does not forget."

" I'll have to have a course of some kind," said Nick. " You're giving me quite an inferiority complex."

" That is impossible. *Au revoir, Mademoiselle.*" He looked round the room. " Your flowers are lovely."

" Aren't they ? The carnations are from Freddie and the roses from George and the lilies from Jim Lazarus. And look here——"

She pulled the wrapping from a large basket of hothouse grapes by her side.

Poirot's face changed. He stepped forward sharply.

" You have not eaten any of them ? "

" No. Not yet."

" Do not do so. You must eat nothing, Mademoiselle, that comes in from outside. *Nothing.* You comprehend ? "

" Oh ! "

She stared at him, the colour ebbing slowly from her face.

" I see. You think—you think it isn't over yet. You think that they're still trying ? " she whispered.

He took her hand.

" Do not think of it. You are safe here. But remember—nothing that comes in from outside."

I was conscious of that white frightened face on the pillow as we left the room.

Poirot looked at his watch.

" *Bon.* We have just time to catch M. Vyse at his office before he leaves it for lunch."

On arrival we were shown into Charles Vyse's office after the briefest of delays.

The young lawyer rose to greet us. He was as formal and unemotional as ever.

" Good-morning, M. Poirot. What can I do for you ? "

Without more ado Poirot presented the letter Nick had written. He took it and read it, then gazed over the top of it at us in a perplexed manner.

" I beg your pardon. I really am at a loss to understand ? "

" Has not Mademoiselle Buckley made her meaning clear ? "

" In this letter," he tapped it with his finger-nail, " she asks me to hand over to you a will made by her and entrusted to my keeping in February last."

" Yes, Monsieur."

" But, my dear sir, no will has been entrusted to my keeping ! "

" *Comment ?* "

" As far as I know my cousin never made a will. I certainly never made one for her."

" She wrote this herself, I understand, on a sheet of notepaper and posted it to you."

The lawyer shook his head.

" In that case all I can say is that I never received it."

" Really, M. Vyse——"

" I never received anything of the kind, M. Poirot."

There was a pause, then Poirot rose to his feet.

" In that case, M. Vyse, there is nothing more to be said. There must be some mistake."

" Certainly there must be some mistake."

He rose also.

" Good-day, M. Vyse."

" Good-day. M. Poirot."

" And that is that," I remarked, when we were out in the street once more.

" *Précisément.*"

" Is he lying, do you think ? "

" Impossible to tell. He has the good poker face, M. Vyse, besides looking as though he had swallowed one. One thing is clear, he will not budge from the position he has taken up. *He never received the will.* That is his point."

" Surely Nick will have a written acknowledgment of its receipt."

" *Cette petite*, she would never bother her head about a thing like that. She despatched it. It was off her mind. *Voilà.* Besides, on that very day, she went into a nursing home to have her appendix out. She had her emotions, in all probability."

" Well, what do we do now ? "

" *Parbleu*, we go and see M. Croft. Let us see what he can remember about this business. It seems to have been very much his doing."

" He didn't profit by it in any way," I said, thoughtfully.

" No. No, I cannot see anything in it from his point of view. He is probably merely the busybody —the man who likes to arrange his neighbour's affairs."

Such an attitude was indeed typical of Mr. Croft, I felt. He was the kindly knowall who causes so much exasperation in this world of ours.

We found him busy in his shirt sleeves over a steaming pot in the kitchen. A most savoury smell pervaded the little lodge.

He relinquished his cookery with enthusiasm, being clearly eager to talk about the murder.

" Half a jiffy," he said. " Walk upstairs. Mother will want to be in on this. She'd never forgive us for talking down here. Cooee—Milly. Two friends coming up."

Mrs. Croft greeted us warmly and was eager for news of Nick. I liked her much better than her husband.

" That poor dear girl," she said. " In a nursing home, you say ? Had a complete breakdown, I shouldn't wonder. A dreadful business, M. Poirot— perfectly dreadful. An innocent young girl like that shot dead. It doesn't bear thinking about—it doesn't indeed. And no lawless wild part of the world either. Right here in the heart of the old country. Kept me awake all night, it did."

" It's made me nervous about going out and leaving you, old lady," said her husband, who had put on his coat and joined us. " I don't like to think of your having been left all alone here yesterday evening. It gives me the shivers."

" You're not going to leave me again, I can tell you," said Mrs. Croft. " Not after dark, anyway. And I'm thinking I'd like to leave this part of the world as soon as possible. I shall never feel the same about it. I shouldn't think poor Nicky Buckley could ever bear to sleep in that house again."

It was a little difficult to reach the object of our visit. Both Mr. and Mrs. Croft talked so much and were so anxious to know all about everything. Were the poor dead girl's relations coming down ? When was the funeral ? Was there to be an inquest ? What did the police think ? Had they any clue yet ? Was it true that a man had been arrested in Plymouth ?

Then, having answered all these questions, they were insistent on offering us lunch. Only Poirot's mendacious statement that we were obliged to hurry back to lunch with the Chief Constable saved us.

At last a momentary pause occurred and Poirot got in the question he had been waiting to ask.

" Why, of course," said Mr. Croft. He pulled the blind cord up and down twice, frowning at it abstractedly. " I remember all about it. Must have been when we first came here. I remember. Appendicitis—that's what the doctor said——"

" And probably not appendicitis at all," interrupted Mrs. Croft. " These doctors—they always like cutting you up if they can. It wasn't the kind you *have* to operate on anyhow. She'd had indigestion and one thing and another, and they'd X-rayed her and they said out it had better come. And there she was, poor little soul, just going off to one of those nasty Homes."

" I just asked her," said Mr. Croft, " if she'd made a will. More as a joke than anything else."

" Yes ? "

" And she wrote it out then and there. Talked about getting a will form at the post office—but I advised her not to. Lot of trouble they cause sometimes, so a man told me. Anyway, her cousin is a lawyer. He could draw her out a proper one afterwards if everything was all right—as, of course, I knew it would be. This was just a precautionary matter."

" Who witnessed it ? "

" Oh ! Ellen, the maid, and her husband."

" And afterwards ? What was done with it ? "

" Oh ! we posted it to Vyse. The lawyer, you know."

" You know that it was posted ? "

" My dear M. Poirot, I posted it myself. Right in this box here by the gate."

" So if M. Vyse says he never got it——"

Croft stared.

" Do you mean that it got lost in the post ? Oh ! but surely that's impossible."

" Anyway, you are certain that you posted it."

" Certain sure," said Mr. Croft, heartily. " I'll take my oath on that any day."

" Ah ! well," said Poirot. " Fortunately it does not matter. Mademoiselle is not likely to die just yet awhile."

" *Et voilà !* " said Poirot, when we were out of earshot and walking down to the hotel. " Who is lying ? M. Croft ? Or M. Charles Vyse ? I must confess I see no reason why M. Croft should be lying. To suppress the will would be of no advantage to him—especially when he had been instrumental in getting it made. No, his statement seems clear enough and tallies exactly with what was told us by Mademoiselle Nick. But all the same——"

" Yes ? "

" All the same, I am glad that M. Croft was doing the cooking when we arrived. He left an excellent impression of a greasy thumb and first finger on a corner of the newspaper that covered the kitchen table. I managed to tear it off unseen by him. We will send it to our good friend Inspector Japp of Scotland Yard. There is just a chance that he might know something about it."

" Yes ? "

" You know, Hastings, I cannot help feeling that our genial M. Croft is a little too good to be genuine."

" And now," he added. " *Le déjeuner*. I faint with hunger."

CHAPTER XV

STRANGE BEHAVIOUR OF FREDERICA

POIROT'S inventions about the Chief Constable were proved not to have been so mendacious after all. Colonel Weston called upon us soon after lunch.

He was a tall man of military carriage with considerable good-looks. He had a suitable reverence for Poirot's achievements, with which he seemed to be well acquainted.

" Marvellous piece of luck for us having you down here, M. Poirot," he said again and again.

His one fear was that he should be compelled to call in the assistance of Scotland Yard. He was anxious to solve the mystery and catch the criminal without their aid. Hence his delight at Poirot's presence in the neighbourhood.

Poirot, so far as I could judge, took him completely into his confidence.

" Deuced odd business," said the Colonel. " Never heard of anything like it. Well, the girl ought to be safe enough in a nursing home. Still, you can't keep her there for ever ! "

" That, M. le Colonel, is just the difficulty. There is only one way of dealing with it."

" And that is ? "

" We must lay our hands on the person responsible."

168

" If what you suspect is true, that isn't going to be so easy."

" *Ah ! je le sais bien.*"

" Evidence ! Getting evidence is going to be the devil."

He frowned abstractedly.

" Always difficult, these cases, where there's no routine work. If we could get hold of the pistol——"

" In all probability it is at the bottom of the sea. That is, if the murderer had any sense."

" Ah ! " said Colonel Weston. " But often they haven't. You'd be surprised at the fool things people do. I'm not talking of murders—we don't have many murders down in these parts, I'm glad to say —but in ordinary police court cases. The sheer damn foolishness of these people would surprise you."

" They are of a different mentality, though."

" Yes—perhaps. If Vyse is the chap, well, we'll have our work cut out. He's a cautious man and a sound lawyer. He'll not give himself away. The woman—well, there would be more hope there. Ten to one she'll try again. Women have no patience."

He rose.

" Inquest to-morrow morning. Coroner will work in with us and give away as little as possible. We want to keep things dark at present."

He was turning towards the door when he suddenly came back.

" Upon my soul, I'd forgotten the very thing that will interest you most, and that I want your opinion about."

Sitting down again, he drew from his pocket a torn scrap of paper with writing on it and handed it to Poirot.

" My police found this when they were searching the grounds. Not far from where you were all watching the fireworks. It's the only suggestive thing they did find."

Poirot smoothed it out. The writing was large and straggling.

" . . . *must have money at once. If not you . . . what will happen. I'm warning you.*"

Poirot frowned. He read and re-read it.

" This is interesting," he said. " I may keep it ? "

" Certainly. There are no fingerprints on it. I'll be glad if you can make anything of it."

Colonel Weston got to his feet again.

" I really must be off. Inquest to-morrow, as I said. By the way, you are not being called as witness —only Captain Hastings. Don't want the newspaper people to get wise to your being on the job."

" I comprehend. What of the relations of the poor young lady ? "

" The father and mother are coming from Yorkshire to-day. They'll arrive about half-past five. Poor souls. I'm heartily sorry for them. They are taking the body back with them the following day."

He shook his head.

" Unpleasant business. I'm not enjoying this, M. Poirot."

"Who could, M. le Colonel ? It is, as you say, an unpleasant business."

When he had gone, Poirot examined the scrap of paper once more.

"An important clue ? " I asked.

He shrugged his shoulders.

"How can one tell ? There is a hint of blackmail about it ! Someone of our party that night was being pressed for money in a very unpleasant way. Of course, it is possible that it was one of the strangers."

He looked at the writing through a little magnifying glass.

"Does this writing look at all familiar to you, Hastings ? "

"It reminds me a little of something—Ah ! I have it—that note of Mrs. Rice's."

"Yes," said Poirot, slowly. "There are resemblances. Decidedly there are resemblances. It is curious. Yet I do not think that this is the writing of Madame Rice. Come in," he said, as a knock came at the door.

It was Commander Challenger.

"Just looked in," he explained. "Wanted to know if you were any further forward."

"*Parbleu*," said Poirot. "At this moment I am feeling that I am considerably further back. I seem to progress *en reculant*."

"That's bad. But I don't really believe it, M. Poirot. I've been hearing all about you and what a wonderful chap you are. Never had a failure, they say."

"That is not true," said Poirot. "I had a bad

failure in Belgium in 1893. You recollect, Hastings ? I recounted it to you. The affair of the box of choco- lates."

" I remember," I said.

And I smiled, for at the time that Poirot told me that tale, he had instructed me to say " chocolate box " to him if ever I should fancy he was growing conceited ! He was then bitterly offended when I used the magical words only a minute and a quarter later.

" Oh, well," said Challenger, " that is such a long time ago it hardly counts. You are going to get to the bottom of this, aren't you ? "

" That I swear. On the word of Hercule Poirot. I am the dog who stays on the scent and does not leave it."

" Good. Got any ideas ? "

" I have suspicions of two people."

" I suppose I mustn't ask who they are ? "

" I should not tell you ! You see, I might possibly be in error."

" *My alibi* is satisfactory, I trust," said Challenger, with a faint twinkle.

Poirot smiled indulgently at the bronzed face in front of him. " You left Devonport at a few minutes past 8.30. You arrived here at five minutes past ten —twenty minutes after the crime had been com- mitted. But the distance from Devonport is only just over thirty miles, and you have often done it in an hour since the road is good. So, you see, your alibi is not good at all ! "

" Well, I'm——"

" You comprehend, I inquire into everything. Your *alibi*, as I say, is not good. But there are other things beside alibis. You would like, I think, to marry Mademoiselle Nick ? "

The sailor's face flushed.

" I've always wanted to marry her," he said huskily.

" Precisely. *Eh bien*—Mademoiselle Nick was engaged to another man. A reason, perhaps, for killing the other man. But that is unnecessary— he dies the death of a hero."

" So it *is* true—that Nick was engaged to Michael Seton ? There's a rumour to that effect all over the town this morning."

" Yes—it is interesting how soon news spreads. You never suspected it before ? "

" I knew Nick was engaged to someone—she told me so two days ago. But she didn't give me a clue as to whom it was."

" It was Michael Seton. *Entre nous*, he has left her, I fancy, a very pretty fortune. Ah ! assuredly, it is not a moment for killing Mademoiselle Nick— from your point of view. She weeps for her lover now, but the heart consoles itself. She is young. And I think, Monsieur, that she is very fond of you. . . ."

Challenger was silent for a moment or two.

" If it should be. . . ." he murmured.

There was a tap on the door.

It was Frederica Rice.

" I've been looking for you," she said to Challenger. " They told me you were here. I

wanted to know if you'd got my wrist-watch back
yet."

" Oh, yes, I called for it this morning."

He took it from his pocket and handed it to her.
It was a watch of rather an unusual shape—round,
like a globe, set on a strap of plain black moire.
I remembered that I had seen one much the same
shape on Nick Buckley's wrist.

" I hope it will keep better time now."

" It's rather a bore. Something is always going
wrong with it."

" It is for beauty, Madame, and not for utility,"
said Poirot.

" Can't one have both ? " She looked from one
to the other of us. "Am I interrupting a confer-
ence?"

" No, indeed, Madame. We were talking the gossip
—not the crime. We were saying how quickly news
spreads—how that everyone now knows that
Mademoiselle Nick was engaged to that brave airman
who perished."

" So Nick *was* engaged to Michael Seton ! " exclaimed Frederica.

" It surprises you, Madame ? "

" It does a little. I don't know why. Certainly I
did think he was very taken with her last autumn.
They went about a lot together. And then, after
Christmas, they both seemed to cool off. As far as I
know, they hardly met."

" The secret, they kept it very well."

" That was because of old Sir Matthew, I suppose.
He was really a little off his head, I think."

" You had no suspicion, Madame ? And yet Mademoiselle was such an intimate friend."

" Nick's a close little devil when she likes," murmured Frederica. " But I understand now why she's been so nervy lately. Oh ! and I ought to have guessed from something she said only the other day."

" Your little friend is very attractive, Madame."

" Old Jim Lazarus used to think so at one time," said Challenger, with his loud, rather tactless laugh.

" Oh ! Jim——" She shrugged her shoulders, but I thought she was annoyed.

She turned to Poirot.

" Tell me, M. Poirot, did you—— ? "

She stopped. Her tall figure swayed and her face turned whiter still. Her eyes were fixed on the centre of the table.

" You are not well, Madame."

I pushed forward a chair, helped her to sink into it. She shook her head, murmured, " I'm all right," and leaned forward, her face between her hands. We watched her awkwardly.

She sat up in a minute.

" How absurd ! George, darling, don't look so worried. Let's talk about murders. Something exciting. I want to know if M. Poirot is on the track."

" It is early to say, Madame," said Poirot, non-committally.

" But you have ideas—yes ? "

" Perhaps. But I need a great deal more evidence."

" Oh ! " She sounded uncertain.

Suddenly she rose.

" I've got a head. I think I'll go and lie down. Perhaps to-morrow they'll let me see Nick."

She left the room abruptly. Challenger frowned.

" You never know what that woman's up to. Nick may have been fond of her, but I don't believe she was fond of Nick. But there, you can't tell with women. It's darling—darling—darling—all the time —and ' damn you ' would probably express it much better. Are you going out, M. Poirot ? " For Poirot had risen and was carefully brushing a speck off his hat.

" Yes, I am going into the town."

" I've got nothing to do. May I come with you."

" Assuredly. It will be a pleasure."

We left the room. Poirot, with an apology, went back.

" My stick," he explained, as he rejoined us.

Challenger winced slightly. And indeed the stick, with its embossed gold band, was somewhat ornate.

Poirot's first visit was to a florist.

" I must send some flowers to Mademoiselle Nick," he explained.

He proved difficult to suit.

In the end he chose an ornate gold basket to be filled with orange carnations. The whole to be tied up with a large blue bow.

The shopwoman gave him a card and he wrote on it with a flourish : " With the Compliments of Hercule Poirot."

" I sent her some flowers this morning," said Challenger. " I might send her some fruit."

" *Inutile !* " said Poirot.

" What ? "

" I said it was useless. The eatables—it is not permitted."

" Who says so ? "

" I say so. I have made the rule. It has already been impressed on Mademoiselle Nick. She understands."

" Good Lord ! " said Challenger.

He looked thoroughly startled. He stared at Poirot curiously.

" So that's it, is it ? " he said. " You're still—afraid."

CHAPTER XVI

INTERVIEW WITH MR. WHITFIELD

THE inquest was a dry proceeding—mere bare bones. There was evidence of identification, then I gave evidence of the finding of the body. Medical evidence followed.

The inquest was adjourned for a week.

The St. Loo murder had jumped into prominence in the daily press. It had, in fact, succeeded " Seton Still Missing. Unknown Fate of Missing Airman."

Now that Seton was dead and due tribute had been paid to his memory, a new sensation was due. The St. Loo Mystery was a godsend to papers at their wits' end for news in the month of August.

After the inquest, having successfully dodged reporters, I met Poirot, and we had an interview with the Rev. Giles Buckley and his wife.

Maggie's father and mother were a charming pair, completely unworldly and unsophisticated.

Mrs. Buckley was a woman of character, tall and fair and showing very plainly her northern ancestry. Her husband was a small man, grey-headed, with a diffident appealing manner.

Poor souls, they were completely dazed by the misfortune that had overtaken them and robbed them of a well-beloved daughter. " Our Maggie," as they called her.

" I can scarcely realise it even now," said Mr. Buckley. " Such a dear child, M. Poirot. So quiet and unselfish—always thinking of others. Who could wish to harm her ? "

" I could hardly understand the telegram," said Mrs. Buckley. " Why, it was only the morning before that we had seen her off."

" In the midst of life we are in death," murmured her husband.

" Colonel Weston has been very kind," said Mrs. Buckley. " He assures us that everything is being done to find the man who did this thing. He must be a madman. No other explanation is possible."

" Madame, I cannot tell you how I sympathise with you in your loss—and how I admire your bravery ! "

" Breaking down would not bring Maggie back to us," said Mrs. Buckley, sadly.

" My wife is wonderful," said the clergyman. " Her faith and courage are greater than mine. It is all so— so bewildering, M. Poirot."

" I know—I know, Monsieur."

" You are a great detective, M. Poirot ? " said Mrs. Buckley.

" It has been said, Madame."

" Oh ! I know. Even in our remote country village we have heard of you. You are going to find out the truth, M. Poirot ? "

" I shall not rest until I do, Madame."

" It will be revealed to you, M. Poirot," quavered the clergyman. " Evil cannot go unpunished."

" Evil never goes unpunished, Monsieur. But the punishment is sometimes secret."

" What do you mean by that, M. Poirot ? "

Poirot only shook his head.

" Poor little Nick," said Mrs. Buckley. " I am really sorriest of all for her. I had a most pathetic letter. She says she feels she asked Maggie down here to her death."

" That is morbid," said Mr. Buckley.

" Yes, but I know how she feels. I wish they would let me see her. It seems so extraordinary not to let her own family visit her."

" Doctors and nurses are very strict," said Poirot, evasively. " They make the rules—so—and nothing will change them. And doubtless they fear for her the emotion—the natural emotion—she would experience on seeing you."

" Perhaps," said Mrs. Buckley, doubtfully. " But I don't hold with nursing homes. Nick would do much better if they let her come back with me—right away from this place."

" It is possible—but I fear they will not agree. It is long since you have seen Mademoiselle Buckley ? "

" I haven't seen her since last autumn. She was at Scarborough. Maggie went over and spent the day with her and then she came back and spent a night with us. She's a pretty creature—though I can't say I like her friends. And the life she leads—well, it's hardly her fault, poor child. She's had no upbringing of any kind."

" It is a strange house—End House," said Poirot, thoughtfully.

" I don't like it," said Mrs. Buckley. " I never have. There's something all wrong about that house.

I disliked old Sir Nicholas intensely. He made me shiver."

" Not a good man, I'm afraid," said her husband. " But he had a curious charm."

" *I* never felt it," said Mrs. Buckley. " There's an evil feeling about that house. I wish we'd never let our Maggie go there."

" Ah l wishing," said Mr. Buckley, and shook his head.

" Well," said Poirot. " I must not intrude upon you any longer. I only wished to proffer to you my deep sympathy."

" You have been very kind, M. Poirot. And we are indeed grateful for all you are doing."

" You return to Yorkshire—when ? "

" To-morrow. A sad journey. Good-bye, M. Poirot, and thank you again."

" Very simple delightful people," I said, after we had left.

Poirot nodded.

" It makes the heart ache, does it not, *mon ami* ? A tragedy so useless—so purposeless. *Cette jeune fille*— Ah l but I reproach myself bitterly. I, Hercule Poirot, was on the spot and I did not prevent the crime ! "

" Nobody could have prevented it."

" You speak without reflection, Hastings. No ordinary person could have prevented it—but of what good is it to be Hercule Poirot with grey cells of a finer quality than other people's, if you do not manage to do what ordinary people cannot ? "

" Well, of course," I said. " If you are going to put it like that——"

" Yes, indeed. I am abashed, downhearted—completely abased."

I reflected that Poirot's abasement was strangely like other people's conceit, but I prudently forebore from making any remark.

" And now," he said, " *en avant. To London.*"

" London ? "

" *Mais oui.* We shall catch the two o'clock train very comfortably. All is peaceful here. Mademoiselle is safe in the nursing home. No one can harm her. The watchdogs, therefore, can take leave of absence. There are one or two little pieces of information that I require."

Our first proceeding on arriving in London was to call upon the late Captain Seton's solicitors, Messrs. Whitfield, Pargiter & Whitfield.

Poirot had arranged for an appointment beforehand, and although it was past six o'clock, we were soon closeted with Mr. Whitfield, the head of the firm.

He was a very urbane and impressive person. He had in front of him a letter from the Chief Constable and another from some high official at Scotland Yard.

" This is all very irregular and unusual, M.—ah—Poirot," he said, as he polished his eyeglasses.

" Quite so, M. Whitfield. But then murder is also irregular—and, I am glad to say, sufficiently unusual."

" True. True. But rather far-fetched—to make a connection between this murder and my late client's bequest—eh ? "

" I think not."

" Ah ! you think not. Well—under the circumstances—and I must admit that Sir Henry puts it very strongly in his letter—I shall be—er—happy to do anything that is in my power."

" You acted as legal adviser to the late Captain Seton ? "

" To all the Seton family, my dear sir. We have done so—our firm have done so, I mean—for the last hundred years."

" *Parfaitement.* The late Sir Matthew Seton made a will ? "

" We made it for him."

" And he left his fortune—how ? "

" There were several bequests—one to the Natural History Museum—but the bulk of his large—his, I may say, *very* large fortune—he left to Captain Michael Seton absolutely. He had no other near relations."

" A very large fortune, you say ? "

" The late Sir Matthew was the second richest man in England," replied Mr. Whitfield, composedly.

" He had somewhat peculiar views, had he not ? "

Mr. Whitfield looked at him severely.

" A millionaire, M. Poirot, is allowed to be eccentric. It is almost expected of him."

Poirot received this correction meekly and asked another question.

" His death was unexpected, I understand ? "

" *Most* unexpected. Sir Matthew enjoyed remarkably good health. He had an internal growth, however, which no one had suspected. It reached a vital tissue and an immediate operation was necessary. The operation was, as always on these occasions, completely successful. But Sir Matthew died."

" And his fortune passed to Captain Seton."

" That is so."

" Captain Seton had, I understand, made a will before leaving England ? "

" If you can call it a will—yes," said Mr. Whitfield, with strong distaste.

" It is legal ? "

" It is perfectly legal. The intention of the testator is plain and it is properly witnessed. Oh, yes, it is legal."

" But you do not approve of it ? "

" My dear sir, what are *we* for ? "

I had often wondered. Having once had occasion to make a perfectly simple will myself, I had been appalled at the length and verbiage that resulted from my solicitor's office.

" The truth of the matter was," continued Mr. Whitfield, " that at the time Captain Seton had little or nothing to leave. He was dependent on the allowance he received from his uncle. He felt, I suppose, that anything would do."

And had thought correctly, I whispered to myself.

" And the terms of this will ? " asked Poirot.

" He leaves everything of which he dies possessed to his affianced wife, Miss Magdala Buckley absolutely. He names me as his executor."

" Then Miss Buckley inherits ? "

" Certainly Miss Buckley inherits."

" And if Miss Buckley had happened to die last Monday ? "

" Captain Seton having predeceased her, the money would go to whoever she had named in her will as residuary legatee—or failing a will to her next of kin."

" I may say," added Mr. Whitfield, with an air of enjoyment, " that the death duties would have been enormous. Enormous ! Three deaths, remember, in rapid succession." He shook his head. " Enormous!"

" But there would have been something left ? " murmured Poirot, meekly.

" My dear sir, as I told you, Sir Matthew was the second richest man in England."

Poirot rose.

" Thank you, Mr. Whitfield, very much for the information that you have given me."

" Not at all. Not at all. I may say that I shall be in communication with Miss Buckley—indeed, I believe the letter has already gone. I shall be happy to be of any service I can to her."

" She is a young lady," said Poirot, " who could do with some sound legal advice."

" There will be fortune hunters, I am afraid," said Mr. Whitfield, shaking his head.

" It seems indicated," agreed Poirot. " Good-day, Monsieur."

" Good-bye, M. Poirot. Glad to have been of service to you. Your name is—ah !—familiar to me."

He said this kindly—with an air of one making a valuable admission.

" It is all exactly as you thought, Poirot," I said, when we were outside.

" *Mon ami*, it was bound to be. *It could not be any other way*. We will go now to the Cheshire Cheese where Japp meets us for an early dinner."

We found Inspector Japp of Scotland Yard awaiting us at the chosen rendezvous. He greeted Poirot with every sign of warmth.

" Years since I've seen you, Moosior Poirot ? Thought you were growing vegetable marrows in the country."

" I tried, Japp, I tried. But even when you grow vegetable marrows you cannot get away from murder."

He sighed. I knew of what he was thinking—that strange affair at Fernley Park. How I regretted that I had been far away at that time.

" And Captain Hastings too," said Japp. " How are you, sir ? "

" Very fit, thanks," I said.

" And now there are more murders ? " continued Japp, facetiously.

" As you say—more murders."

" Well, you mustn't be depressed, old cock," said Japp. " Even if you can't see your way clear—well —you can't go about at your time of life and expect to have the success you used to do. We all of us get stale as the years go by. Got to give the young 'uns a chance, you know."

" And yet the old dog is the one who knows the tricks," murmured Poirot. " He is cunning. He does not leave the scent."

" Oh ! well—we're talking about human beings, not dogs."

" Is there so much difference ? "

" Well, it depends how you look at things. But you're a caution, isn't he, Captain Hastings ? Always was. Looks much the same—hair a bit thinner on top but the face fungus fuller than ever."

" Eh ? " said Poirot. " What is that ? "

" He's congratulating you on your moustaches," I said, soothingly.

" They are luxuriant, yes," said Poirot, complacently caressing them.

Japp went off into a roar of laughter.

" Well," he said, after a minute or two, " I've done your bit of business. Those fingerprints you sent me——"

" Yes ? " said Poirot, eagerly.

" Nothing doing. Whoever the gentleman may be—he hasn't passed through *our* hands. On the other hand, I wired to Melbourne and nobody of that description or name is known there."

" Ah ! "

" So there may be something fishy after all. But he's not one of the lads."

" As to the other business," went on Japp.

" Yes ? "

" Lazarus and Son have a good reputation. Quite straight and honourable in their dealings. Sharp, of course—but that's another matter. You've got to be sharp in business. But they're all right. They're in a bad way, though—financially, I mean."

" Oh !—is that so ? "

" Yes—the slump in pictures has hit them badly. And antique furniture too. All this modern continental stuff coming into fashion. They built new premises last year and—well—as I say, they're not far from Queer Street."

" I am much obliged to you."

" Not at all. That sort of thing isn't my line, as you know. But I made a point of finding out as you wanted to know. We can always get information."

" My good Japp, what should I do without you ? "

" Oh ! that's all right. Always glad to oblige an old friend. I let you in on some pretty good cases in the old days, didn't I ? "

This, I realised, was Japp's way of acknowledging indebtedness to Poirot, who had solved many a case which had baffled the Inspector.

" They were the good days—yes."

" I wouldn't mind having a chat with you now and again even in these days. Your methods may be old-fashioned but you've got your head screwed on the right way, M. Poirot."

" What about my other question. The Dr. MacAllister ? "

" Oh, him ! He's a woman's doctor. I don't mean a gynecologist. I mean one of these nerve doctors—tell you to sleep in purple walls and an orange ceiling —talk to you about your libido, whatever that is—tell you to let it rip. He's a bit of a quack, if you ask me—but he gets the women all right. They flock to him. Goes abroad a good deal—does some kind of medical work in Paris, I believe."

" Why Dr. MacAllister ? " I asked, bewildered.

I had never heard of the name. " Where does he come in ? "

" Dr. MacAllister is the uncle of Commander Challenger," explained Poirot. " You remember he referred to an uncle who was a doctor ? "

" How thorough you are," I said. " Did you think he had operated on Sir Matthew ? "

" He's not a surgeon," said Japp.

" *Mon ami*," said Poirot, " I like to inquire into everything. Hercule Poirot is a good dog. The good dog follows the scent, and if, regrettably, there is no scent to follow, he noses around—seeking always something that is not very nice. So also, does Hercule Poirot. And often—oh ! so often—does he find it ! "

" It's not a nice profession, ours," said Japp. " Stilton, did you say ? I don't mind if I do. No, it's not a nice profession. And yours is worse than mine—not official, you see, and therefore a lot more worming yourself into places in underhand ways."

" I do not disguise myself, Japp. Never have I disguised myself."

" You couldn't," said Japp. " You're unique. Once seen, never forgotten."

Poirot looked at him rather doubtfully.

" Only my fun," said Japp. " Don't mind me. Glass of port ? Well, if you say so."

The evening became thoroughly harmonious. We were soon in the middle of reminiscences. This case, that case, and the other. I must say that I, too, enjoyed talking over the past. Those had been good days. How old and experienced I felt now !

Poor old Poirot. He was perplexed by this case—

I could see that. His powers were not what they were. I had the feeling that he was going to fail—that the murderer of Maggie Buckley would never be brought to book.

"Courage, my friend," said Poirot, slapping me on the shoulder. "All is not lost. Do not pull the long face, I beg of you."

"That's all right. I'm all right."

"And so am I. And so is Japp."

"We're all all right," declared Japp, hilariously.

And on this pleasant note we parted.

The following morning we journeyed back to St. Loo. On arrival at the hotel Poirot rang up the nursing home and asked to speak to Nick.

Suddenly I saw his face change—he almost dropped the instrument.

"*Comment?* What is that? Say it again, I beg."

He waited for a minute or two listening. Then he said :

"Yes, yes, I will come at once."

He turned a pale face to me.

"Why did I go away, Hastings? *Mon Dieu!* Why did I go away?"

"What has happened?"

"Mademoiselle Nick is dangerously ill. Cocaine poisoning. They have got at her after all. *Mon Dieu! Mon Dieu! why did I go away?*"

CHAPTER XVII

A BOX OF CHOCOLATES

ALL the way to the nursing home Poirot murmured and muttered to himself. He was full of self-reproach.

"I should have known," he groaned. "I should have known! And yet, what could I do? I took every precaution. It is impossible—impossible. *No one* could get to her! Who has disobeyed my orders?"

At the nursing home we were shown into a little room downstairs, and after a few minutes Dr. Graham came to us. He looked exhausted and white.

"She'll do," he said. "It's going to be all right. The trouble was knowing how much she'd taken of the damned stuff."

"What was it?"

"Cocaine."

"She will live?"

"Yes, yes, she'll live."

"But how did it happen? How did they get at her? Who has been allowed in?" Poirot fairly danced with impotent excitement.

"Nobody has been allowed in."

"Impossible."

"It's true."

"But then——"

" It was a box of chocolates."

" Ah ! *sacré*. And I told her to eat *nothing—nothing*—that came from outside."

" I don't know about that. It's hard work keeping a girl from a box of chocolates. She only ate one, thank goodness."

" Was there cocaine in all the chocolates ? "

" No. The girl ate one. There were two others in the top layer. The rest were all right."

" How was it done ? "

" Quite clumsily. Chocolate cut in half—the cocaine mixed with the filling and the chocolate stuck together again. Amateurishly. What you might call a home-made job."

Poirot groaned.

" Ah ! if I knew—if I knew. Can I see Mademoiselle ? "

" If you come back in an hour I think you can see her," said the doctor. " Pull yourself together, man. She isn't going to die."

For another hour we walked the streets of St. Loo. I did my best to distract Poirot's mind—pointing out to him that all was well, that, after all, no mischief had been done.

But he only shook his head, and repeated at intervals :

" *I am afraid, Hastings, I am afraid. . . .*"

And the strange way he said it made me, too, feel afraid.

Once he caught me by the arm.

" Listen, my friend. *I am all wrong.* I have been all wrong from the beginning."

" You mean it isn't the money——"

" No, no, I am right about that. Oh, yes. But those two—it is too simple—too easy, that. There is another twist still. Yes, there is something ! "

And then in an outburst of indignation :

" *Ah ! cette petite !* Did I not *forbid* her ? Did I not say, ' Do not touch anything from outside ? ' And she disobeys me—me, Hercule Poirot. Are not four escapes from death enough for her ? Must she take a fifth chance ? *Ah, c'est inoui !* "

At last we made our way back. After a brief wait we were conducted upstairs.

Nick was sitting up in bed. The pupils of her eyes were widely dilated. She looked feverish and her hands kept twitching violently.

" At it again," she murmured.

Poirot experienced real emotion at the sight of her. He cleared his throat and took her hand in his.

" Ah ! Mademoiselle—Mademoiselle."

" I shouldn't care," she said, defiantly, " if they *had* got me this time. I'm sick of it all—sick of it ! "

" *Pauvre petite !* "

" Something in me doesn't like to give them best! "

" That is the spirit—*le sport*—you must be the good sport, Mademoiselle."

" Your old nursing home hasn't been so safe after all," said Nick.

" If you had obeyed orders, Mademoiselle——"

She looked faintly astonished.

" But I have."

" Did I not impress upon you that you were to eat nothing that came from outside ? "

N

" No more I did."

" But these chocolates——"

" Well, they were all right. *You* sent them."

" What is that you say, Mademoiselle ? "

" *You* sent them ! "

" Me ? Never. Never anything of the kind."

" But you *did*. Your card was in the box."

" What ? "

Nick made a spasmodic gesture towards the table by the bed. The nurse came forward.

" You want the card that was in the box ? "

" Yes, please, nurse."

There was a moment's pause. The nurse returned to the room with it in her hand.

" Here it is."

I gasped. So did Poirot. For on the card, in flourishing handwriting, was written the same words that I had seen Poirot inscribe on the card that accompanied the basket of flowers.

" With the Compliments of Hercule Poirot."

" *Sacré tonnerre !* "

" You see," said Nick, accusingly.

" I did not write this ! " cried Poirot.

" What ? "

" And yet," murmured Poirot, " and yet it is my handwriting."

" I know. It's exactly the same as the card that came with the orange carnations. I never doubted that the chocolates came from you."

Poirot shook his head.

" How should you doubt ? Oh ! the devil ! The clever, cruel devil ! To think of *that* ! Ah ! but he has

genius, this man, genius ! ' *With the Compliments of
Hercule Poirot.*' So simple. Yes, but one had to
think of it. And I—I did not *think*. I omitted to
foresee this move."

Nick moved restlessly.

" Do not agitate yourself, Mademoiselle. You are
blameless—blameless. It is I that am to blame,
miserable imbecile that I am ! I should have foreseen this move. Yes, I should have foreseen it."

His chin dropped on his breast. He looked the
picture of misery.

" I really think——" said the nurse.

She had been hovering nearby, a disapproving
expression on her face.

" Eh ? Yes, yes, I will go. Courage, Mademoiselle.
This is the last mistake I will make. I am ashamed,
desolated—I have been tricked, outwitted—as
though I were a little schoolboy. *But it shall not
happen again.* No. I promise you. Come, Hastings."

Poirot's first proceeding was to interview the
matron. She was, naturally, terribly upset over the
whole business.

" It seems incredible to me, M. Poirot, absolutely
incredible. That a thing like that should happen in
my nursing home."

Poirot was sympathetic and tactful. Having
soothed her sufficiently, he began to inquire into the
circumstance of the arrival of the fatal packet. Here,
the matron declared, he would do best to interview
the orderly who had been on duty at the time of its
arrival.

The man in question, whose name was Hood, was

a stupid but honest-looking young fellow of about twenty-two. He looked nervous and frightened. Poirot put him at his ease, however.

" No blame can be attached to you," he said, kindly. " But I want you to tell me exactly when and how this parcel arrived."

The orderly looked puzzled.

" It's difficult to say, sir," he said, slowly. " Lots of people come and inquire and leave things for the different patients."

" The nurse says this came last night," I said. " About six o'clock."

The lad's face brightened.

" I do remember, now, sir. A gentleman brought it."

" A thin-faced gentleman—fair-haired ? "

" He was fair-haired—but I don't know about thin-faced."

" Would Charles Vyse bring it himself ? " I murmured to Poirot.

I had forgotten that the lad would know a local name.

" It wasn't Mr. Vyse," he said. " I know him. It was a bigger gentleman—handsome-looking—came in a big car."

" Lazarus," I exclaimed.

Poirot shot me a warning glance and I regretted my precipitance.

" He came in a large car and he left this parcel. It was addressed to Miss Buckley ? "

" Yes, sir."

" And what did you do with it ? "

" I didn't touch it, sir. Nurse took it up."

" Quite so, but you touched it when you took it from the gentleman, *n'est ce pas* ? "

" Oh ! that, yes, of course, sir. I took it from him and put it on the table."

" Which table ? Show me, if you please."

The orderly led us into the hall. The front door was open. Close to it, in the hall, was a long marble-topped table on which lay letters and parcels.

" Everything that comes is put on here, sir. Then the nurses take things up to the patients."

" Do you remember what time this parcel was left ? "

" Must have been about five-thirty, or a little after. I know the post had just been, and that's usually at about half-past five. It was a pretty busy afternoon, a lot of people leaving flowers and coming to see patients."

" Thank you. Now, I think, we will see the nurse who took up the parcel."

This proved to be one of the probationers, a fluffy little person all agog with excitement. She remembered taking the parcel up at six o'clock when she came on duty.

" Six o'clock," murmured Poirot. " Then it must have been twenty minutes or so that the parcel was lying on the table downstairs."

" Pardon ? "

" Nothing, Mademoiselle. Continue. You took the parcel to Miss Buckley ? "

" Yes, there were several things for her. There was this box and some flowers also—sweet peas—from a

Mr. and Mrs. Croft, I think. I took them up at the same time. And there was a parcel that had come by post—and curiously enough *that* was a box of Fuller's chocolates also."

" *Comment?* A second box ? "

" Yes, rather a coincidence. Miss Buckley opened them both. She said : ' Oh ! what a shame. I'm not allowed to eat them.' Then she opened the lids to look inside and see if they were both just the same, and your card was in one and she said, " Take the other impure box away, nurse. I might get them mixed up.' Oh ! dear, whoever would have thought of such a thing ? Seems like an Edgar Wallace, doesn't it ? "

Poirot cut short this flood of speech.

" Two boxes, you say ? From whom was the other box ? "

" There was no name inside."

" And which was the one that came—that had the appearance of coming—from me ? The one by post or the other ? "

" I declare now—I can't remember. Shall I go up and ask Miss Buckley ? "

" If you would be so amiable."

She ran up the stairs.

" Two boxes," murmured Poirot. " There is confusion for you."

The nurse returned breathless.

" Miss Buckley isn't sure. She unwrapped them both before she looked inside. But she thinks it wasn't the box that came by post."

" Eh ? " said Poirot, a little confused.

" The box from you was the one that didn't come by post. At least she thinks so, but she isn't quite sure."

" *Diable!* " said Poirot, as we walked away. " Is no one ever quite sure ? In detective books—yes. But life—real life—is always full of muddle. Am I sure, myself, about anything at all ? No, no—a thousand times, no."

" Lazarus," I said.

" Yes, that is a surprise, is it not ? "

" Shall you say anything to him about it ? "

" Assuredly. I shall be interested to see how he takes it. By the way, we might as well exaggerate the serious condition of Mademoiselle. It will do no harm to let it be assumed that she is at death's door. You comprehend ? The solemn face—yes, admirable. You resemble closely an undertaker. *C'est tout à fait bien.*"

We were lucky in finding Lazarus. He was bending over the bonnet of his car outside the hotel.

Poirot went straight up to him.

" Yesterday evening, Monsieur Lazarus, you left a box of chocolates for Mademoiselle," he began, without preamble.

Lazarus looked rather surprised.

" Yes ? "

" That was very amiable of you."

" As a matter of fact they were from Freddie, from Mrs. Rice. She asked me to get them."

" Oh ! I see."

" I took them round there in the car."

" I comprehend."

He was silent for a minute or two and then said :

" Madame Rice, where is she ? "

" I think she's in the lounge."

We found Frederica having tea. She looked up at us with an anxious face.

" What is this I hear about Nick being taken ill ? "

" It is a most mysterious affair, Madame. Tell me, did you send her a box of chocolates yesterday ? "

" Yes. At least she asked me to get them for her."

" *She* asked you to get them for her ? "

" Yes."

" But she was not allowed to see anyone. How did you see her ? "

" I didn't. She telephoned."

" Ah ! And she said—what ? "

" Would I get her a two-pound box of Fuller's chocolates."

" How did her voice sound—weak ? "

" No—not at all. Quite strong. But different somehow. I didn't realise it was she speaking at first."

" Until she told you who she was ? "

" Yes."

" Are you sure, Madame, that it *was* your friend ?

Frederica looked startled.

" I—I—why, of course it was. Who else could it have been ? "

" That is an interesting question, Madame."

" You don't mean——"

" *Could you swear*, Madame, that it was your friend's voice—apart from what she said ? "

" No." said Frederica. slowly, " I couldn't. Her

voice was certainly different. I thought it was the phone—or perhaps being ill. . . ."

" If she had not told you who she was, you would not have recognised it ? "

" No, no, I don't think I should. Who was it, M. Poirot ? Who was it ? "

" That is what I mean to know, Madame."

The graveness of his face seemed to awaken her suspicions.

" Is Nick—has anything happened ? " she asked, breathlessly.

Poirot nodded.

" She is ill—dangerously ill. Those chocolates, Madame—were poisoned."

" The chocolates *I* sent her ? But that's impossible—impossible ! "

" Not impossible, Madame, since Mademoiselle is at death's door."

" Oh, my God." She hid her face in her hands, then raised it white and quivering. " I don't understand—I don't understand. The other, yes, but not this. They couldn't be poisoned. Nobody ever touched them but me and Jim. You're making some dreadful mistake, M. Poirot."

" It is not I that make a mistake—even though my name was in the box."

She stared at him blankly.

" If Mademoiselle Nick dies——" he said, and made a threatening gesture with his hand.

She gave a low cry.

He turned away, and taking me by the arm, went up to the sitting-room.

He flung his hat on the table.

" I understand nothing—but nothing ! I am in the dark. I am a little child. Who stands to gain by Mademoiselle's death ? Madame Rice. Who buys the chocolates and admits it and tells a story of being rung up on the telephone that cannot hold water for a minute ? Madame Rice. It is too simple—too stupid. And she is not stupid—no."

" Well, then——"

" But she takes cocaine, Hastings. I am certain she takes cocaine. There is no mistaking it. And there was cocaine in those chocolates. And what does she mean when she said, ' *The other, yes, but not this.*' It needs explaining, that ! And the sleek M. Lazarus—what is *he* doing in all this ? What does she know, Madame Rice ? She knows something. But I cannot make her speak. She is not of those you can frighten into speech. But she knows something, Hastings. Is her tale of the telephone true, or did she invent it ? If it is true, whose voice was it ?

" I tell you, Hastings. This is all very black—very black."

"Always darkest before dawn," I said reassuringly.

He shook his head.

" Then the other box—that came by post. Can we rule that out ? No, we cannot, because Mademoiselle is not sure. It is an annoyance, that ! "

He groaned.

I was about to speak when he stopped me.

" No, no. Not another proverb. I cannot bear it. If you would be the good friend—the good helpful friend——"

" Yes," I said, eagerly.

" Go out, I beg of you, and buy me some playing cards."

I stared.

" Very well," I said coldly.

I could not but suspect that he was making a deliberate excuse to get rid of me.

Here, however, I misjudged him. That night, when I came into the sitting-room about ten o'clock, I found Poirot carefully building card houses—and I remembered !

It was an old trick of his—soothing his nerves. He smiled at me.

" Yes—you remember. One needs the precision. One card on another—so—in exactly the right place and that supports the weight of the card on top and so on, up and up. Go to bed, Hastings. Leave me here, with my house of cards. I clear the mind."

It was about five in the morning when I was shaken awake.

Poirot was standing by my bedside. He looked pleased and happy.

" It was very just what you said, *mon ami*. Oh ! it was very just. More, it was *spirituel* ! "

I blinked at him, being imperfectly awake.

" Always darkest before dawn—that is what you said. It has been very dark—and now it is dawn."

I looked at the window. He was perfectly right.

" No, no, Hastings. In the head ! The mind ! The little grey cells ! "

He paused and then said quietly :

" You see, Hastings, Mademoiselle is dead."

" What ? " I cried, suddenly wide awake.

" Hush—hush. It is as I say. Not really—*bien entendu*—but it can be arranged. Yes, for twenty-four hours it can be arranged. I arrange it with the doctor, with the nurses.

" You comprehend, Hastings ? *The murderer has been successful.* Four times he has tried and failed. The fifth time he has succeeded.

" *And now, we shall see what happens next. . . .*

" It will be very interesting."

CHAPTER XVIII

THE FACE AT THE WINDOW

THE events of the next day are completely hazy in my memory. I was unfortunate enough to awake with fever on me. I have been liable to these bouts of fever at inconvenient times ever since I once contracted malaria.

In consequence, the events of that day take on in my memory the semblance of a nightmare—with Poirot coming and going as a kind of fantastic clown, making a periodic appearance in a circus.

He was, I fancy, enjoying himself to the full. His pose of baffled despair was admirable. How he achieved the end he had in view and which he had disclosed to me in the early hours of the morning, I cannot say. But achieve it he did.

It cannot have been easy. The amount of deception and subterfuge involved must have been colossal. The English character is averse to lying on a wholesale scale and that, no less, was what Poirot's plan required. He had, first, to get Dr. Graham converted to the scheme. With Dr. Graham on his side, he had to persuade the Matron and some members of the staff of the nursing home to conform to the plan. There again, the difficulties must have been immense. It was probably Dr. Graham's influence that turned the scale.

Then there was the Chief Constable and the police.
Here, Poirot would be up against officialdom.
Nevertheless he wrung at last an unwilling consent
out of Colonel Weston. The Colonel made it clear
that it was in no way his responsibility. Poirot and
Poirot alone was responsible for the spreading abroad
of these lying reports. Poirot agreed. He would have
agreed to anything so long as he was permitted to
carry out his plan.

I spent most of the day dozing in a large armchair
with a rug over my knees. Every two or three hours
or so, Poirot would burst in and report progress.

"*Comment ça va, mon ami?* How I commiserate
you. But it is as well, perhaps. The farce, you do not
play it as well as I do. I come this moment from
ordering a wreath—a wreath immense—stupendous.
Lilies, my friend—large quantities of lilies. '*With
heartfelt regret. From Hercule Poirot.*' Ah! what a
comedy."

He departed again.

"I come from a most poignant conversation with
Madame Rice," was his next piece of information.
"Very well dressed in the black, that one. Her poor
friend—what a tragedy! I groan sympathetically.
Nick, she says, was so joyous, so full of life. Impossible to think of her as dead. I agree. 'It is, I
say, the irony of death that it takes one like that.
The old and useless are left.' Oh! *là là!* I groan
again."

"How you are enjoying this," I murmured, feebly.

"*Du tout.* It is part of my plan, that is all. To
play the comedy successfully, you must put the

heart into it. Well, then, the conventional expressions of regret over, Madame comes to matters nearer home. All night she has lain awake wondering about those sweets. It is impossible—impossible. ' Madame,' I say, ' It is not impossible. You can see the analyst's report.' Then she says, and her voice is far from steady, ' It was—*cocaine*, you say ? ' I assent. And she says, ' Oh, my God. I don't understand.' "

" Perhaps that's true."

" She understands well enough that she is in danger. She is intelligent. I told you that before. Yes, she is in danger, and she knows it."

" And yet it seems to me that for the first time you don't believe her guilty."

Poirot frowned. The excitement of his manner abated.

" It is profound what you say there, Hastings. No—it seems to me that—somehow—the facts no longer fit. These crimes—so far what has marked them most—the subtlety, is it not ? And here is no subtlety at all—only the crudity, pure and simple. No, it does not fit."

He sat down at the table.

" *Voilà*—let us examine the facts. There are three possibilities. There are the sweets bought by Madame and delivered by M. Lazarus. And in that case the guilt rests with one or the other or *both*. And the telephone call, supposedly from Mademoiselle Nick, that is an invention pure and simple. That is the straightforward—the obvious solution.

" Solution 2 : The *other* box of sweets—that which

came by post. Anyone may have sent those. Any
of the suspects on our list from A. to J. (You remember ? A very wide field.) But, if that were the
guilty box, *what is the point of the telephone call ?*
Why complicate matters with a second box ? "

I shook my head feebly. With a temperature of
102, any complication seemed to me quite unnecessary and absurd.

" Solution 3 : A poisoned box was substituted for
the innocent box bought by Madame. In that case
the telephone call is ingenious and understandable.
Madame is to be what you call the kitten's paw. She
is to pull the roasting chestnuts out of the fire. So
Solution 3 is the most logical—but, alas, it is also the
most difficult. How be sure of substituting a box at
the right moment ? The orderly might take the box
straight upstairs—a hundred and one possibilities
might prevent the substitution being effected. No,
it does not seem sense."

" Unless it were Lazarus," I said.

Poirot looked at me.

" You have the fever, my friend. It mounts, does
it not ? "

I nodded.

" Curious how a few degrees of heat should stimu-
late the intellect. You have uttered there an observation of profound simplicity. So simple, was it, that
I had failed to consider it. But it would suppose a
very curious state of affairs. M. Lazarus, the dear
friend of Madame, doing his best to get her hanged.
It opens up possibilities of a very curious nature.
But complex—very complex."

I closed my eyes. I was glad I had been brilliant, but I did not want to think of anything complex. I wanted to go to sleep.

Poirot, I think, went on talking, but I did not listen. His voice was vaguely soothing. . . .

It was late afternoon when I saw him next.

"My little plan, it has made the fortune of the flower shops," he announced. "Everybody orders wreaths. M. Croft, M. Vyse, Commander Challenger——"

The last name awoke a chord of compunction in my mind.

"Look here, Poirot," I said. "You must let him in on this. Poor fellow, he will be distracted with grief. It isn't fair."

"You have always the tenderness for him, Hastings."

"I like him. He's a thoroughly decent chap. You've got to take him into the secret."

Poirot shook his head.

"No, *mon ami*. I do not make the exceptions."

"But you don't suspect him of having anything to do with it?"

"I do not make the exceptions."

"Think how he must be suffering."

"On the contrary, I prefer to think of what a joyful surprise I prepare for him. To think the loved one dead—and find her alive! It is a sensation unique—stupendous."

"What a pig-headed old devil you are. He'd keep the secret all right."

"I am not so sure."

" He's the soul of honour. I'm certain of it."

" That makes it all the more difficult to keep a secret. Keeping a secret is an art that requires many lies magnificently told, and a great aptitude for playing the comedy and enjoying it. Could he dissemble, the Commander Challenger? If he is what you say he is, he certainly could *not*."

" Then you won't tell him? "

" I certainly refuse to imperil my little idea for the sake of the sentiment. It is life and death we play with, *mon cher*. Anyway, the suffering, it is good for the character. Many of your famous clergymen have said so—even a Bishop if I am not mistaken."

I made no further attempt to shake his decision. His mind, I could see, was made up.

" I shall not dress for dinner," he murmured. " I am too much the broken old man. That is my part, you understand. All my self-confidence has crashed —I am broken. I have failed. I shall eat hardly any dinner—the food untasted on the plate. That is the attitude, I think. In my own apartment I will consume some brioches and some chocolate *éclairs* (so called) which I had the foresight to buy at a confectioners. *Et vous?* "

" Some more quinine, I think," I said, sadly.

" Alas, my poor Hastings. But courage, all will be well to-morrow."

" Very likely. These attacks often last only twenty-four hours."

I did not hear him return to the room. I must have been asleep.

When I awoke, he was sitting at the table writing.

In front of him was a crumpled sheet of paper smoothed out. I recognised it for the paper on which he had written that list of people—A. to J.—which he had afterwards crumpled up and thrown away.

He nodded in answer to my unspoken thought.

" Yes, my friend. I have resurrected it. I am at work upon it from a different angle. I compile a list of questions concerning each person. The questions may have no bearing on the crime—they are just things that I do not know—things that remain unexplained, and for which I seek to supply the answer from my own brain."

" How far have you got ? "

" I have finished. You would like to hear ? You are strong enough ? "

" Yes, as a matter of fact, I am feeling a great deal better."

" *A la bonheur !* Very well, I will read them to you. Some of them, no doubt, you will consider puerile."

He cleared his throat.

" A. *Ellen.*—Why did she remain in the house and not go out to see fireworks ? (Unusual, as Mademoiselle's evidence and surprise make clear.) What did she think or suspect might happen ? Did she admit anyone (J. for instance) to the house ? Is she speaking the truth about the secret panel ? If there is such a thing why is she unable to remember where it is ? (Mademoiselle seems very certain there is no such thing—and she would surely know.) If she invented it, why

did she invent it ? Had she read Michael
Seton's love letters or was her surprise at
Mademoiselle Nick's engagement genuine ?

" B. *Her Husband.*—Is he as stupid as he seems ?
Does he share Ellen's knowledge whatever
it is, or does he not ? Is he, in any respect,
a mental case ?

" C. *The Child.*—Is his delight in blood a natural
instinct common to his age and develop-
ment, or is it morbid, and is that morbidity
inherited from either parent ? Has he ever
shot with a toy pistol ?

" D. *Who is Mr. Croft ?*—Where does he really
come from ? Did he post the will as he
swears he did ? What motive could he
have in *not* posting it ?

" E. *Same as above.*—Who *are* Mr. and Mrs. Croft ?
Are they in hiding for some reason—and if
so, what reason ? Have they any connection with the Buckley family ?

" F. *Mrs. Rice.*—Was she really aware of the
engagement between Nick and Michael
Seton ? Did she merely guess it, or had
she actually read the letters which passed
between them ? (In that case she would
know Mademoiselle was Seton's heir.) Did
she know that she herself was Mademoiselle's residuary legatee ? (This, I think, is
likely. Mademoiselle would probably tell
her so, adding perhaps that she would not
get much out of it.) Is there any truth
in Commander Challenger's suggestion that

Lazarus was attracted by Mademoiselle Nick ? (This might explain a certain lack of cordiality between the two friends which seems to have shown itself in the last few months.) Who is the ' boy friend' mentioned in her note as supplying the drug ? *Could this possibly be J.?* Why did she turn faint one day in this room ? Was it something that had been said—or was it something she *saw* ? Is her account of the telephone message asking her to buy chocolates correct—or is it a deliberate lie ? What did she mean by' I can understand the other—but not this ? ' If she is not herself guilty, what knowledge has she got that she is keeping to herself ? "

" You perceive," said Poirot, suddenly breaking off, " that the questions concerning Madame Rice are almost innumerable. From beginning to end, she is an enigma. And that forces me to a conclusion. Either Madame Rice is guilty—or she knows—or shall we say, thinks she knows—who *is* guilty. But is she right ? Does she know or does she merely suspect ? And how is it possible to make her speak?"

He sighed.

" Well, I will go on with my list of questions.

" G. *Mr. Lazarus.*—Curious—there are practically no questions to ask concerning him—except the crude one, ' Did he substitute the poisoned sweets ? Otherwise I find only

one totally irrelevant question. But I have
put it down. ' Why did M. Lazarus offer
fifty pounds for a picture that was only
worth twenty ? "

" He wanted to do Nick a good turn," I suggested.
" He would not do it that way. He is a dealer.
He does not buy to sell at a loss. If he wished to be
amiable he would lend her money as a private
individual."
" It can't have any bearing on the crime, anyway."
" No, that is true—but all the same, I should like
to know. I am a student of the psychology, you
understand.
" Now we come to H.

" H. *Commander Challenger.*—Why did Mademoiselle Nick tell him she was engaged to
someone else ? What necessitated her
having to tell him that ? She told no one
else. Had he proposed to her ? What are
his relations with his uncle ? "

" His uncle, Poirot ? "
" Yes, the doctor. That rather questionable
character. Did any private news of Michael Seton's
death come through to the Admiralty before it was
announced publicly ? "
" I don't quite see what you're driving at, Poirot.
Even if Challenger knew beforehand about Seton's
death, it does not seem to get us anywhere. It

provides no earthly motive for killing the girl he loved."

" I quite agree. What you say is perfectly reasonable. But these are just things I should like to know. I am still the dog, you see, nosing about for the things that are not very nice !

" I. *M. Vyse.*—Why did he say what he did about his cousin's fanatical devotion to End House ? What possible motive could he have in saying that ? Did he, or did he not, receive the will ? Is he, in fact, an honest man—or is he not an honest man ?

" *And now J.*—*Eh bien*, J. is what I put down before—a giant question mark. Is there such a person, or is there not——

" *Mon Dieu !* my friend, what have you ? "

I had started from my chair with a sudden shriek. With a shaking hand I pointed at the window.

" A face, Poirot ! " I cried. " A face pressed against the glass. A dreadful face ! It's gone now—but I saw it."

Poirot strode to the window and pushed it open. He leant out.

" There is no one there now," he said, thoughtfully. " You are sure you did not imagine it, Hastings ? "

" Quite sure. It was a horrible face."

" There is a balcony, of course. Anyone could reach there quite easily if they wanted to hear what we were saying. When you say a dreadful face, Hastings, just what do you mean ? "

" A white, staring face, hardly human."

" *Mon ami*, that is the fever. A face, yes. An unpleasant face, yes. But a face hardly human—*no*. What you saw was the effect of a face pressed closely against the glass—that allied to the shock of seeing it there at all."

" It was a dreadful face," I said, obstinately.

" It was not the face of—anyone you know ? "

" No, indeed."

" H'm—it might have been, though ! I doubt if you would recognise it under these circumstances. I wonder now—yes, I very much wonder. . . ."

He gathered up his papers thoughtfully.

" One thing at least is to the good. If the owner of that face overheard our conversation we did not mention that Mademoiselle Nick was alive and well. Whatever else our visitor may have heard, that at least escaped him."

" But surely," I said, " the results of this—er— brilliant manœuvre of yours have been slightly disappointing up to date. Nick is dead and no startling developments have occurred ! "

" I did not expect them yet awhile. Twenty-four hours, I said. *Mon ami*, to-morrow, if I am not mistaken, certain things will arise. Otherwise—otherwise I am wrong from start to finish. There is the post, you see. I have hopes of to-morrow's post."

I awoke in the morning feeling weak but with the fever abated. I also felt hungry. Poirot and I had breakfast served in our sitting-room.

" Well ? " I said, maliciously, as he sorted his letters. " Has the post done what you expected of it ? "

Poirot, who had just opened two envelopes which patently contained bills, did not reply. I thought he looked rather cast down and not his usual cock-a-hoop self.

I opened my own mail. The first was a notice of a spiritualist meeting.

" If all else fails, we must go to the spiritualists," I remarked. " I often wonder that more tests of this kind aren't made. The spirit of the victim comes back and names the murderer. That would be a proof."

" It would hardly help us," said Poirot, absently. " I doubt if Maggie Buckley knew whose hand it was shot her down. Even if she could speak she would have nothing of value to tell us. *Tiens !* that is odd."

" What is ? "

" You talk of the dead speaking, and at that moment I open this letter."

He tossed it across to me. It was from Mrs. Buckley and ran as follows :

" *Langley Rectory.*

" DEAR MONSIEUR POIROT,—On my return here I found a letter written by my poor child on her arrival at St. Loo. There is nothing in it of interest to you, I'm afraid, but I thought perhaps you would care to see it.

" Thanking you for your kindness,
" Yours sincerely,
"JEAN BUCKLEY."

The enclosure brought a lump to my throat. It was so terribly commonplace and so completely untouched by any apprehension of tragedy !

"DEAR MOTHER,—I arrived safely. Quite a comfortable journey. Only two other people in the carriage all the way to Exeter.

"It is lovely weather here. Nick seems very well and gay—a little restless, perhaps, but I cannot see why she should have telegraphed for me in the way she did. Tuesday would have done just as well.

"No more now. We are going to have tea with some neighbours. They are Australians and have rented the lodge. Nick says they are kind but rather awful. Mrs. Rice and Mr. Lazarus are coming to stay. He is the art dealer. I will post this in the box by the gate, then it will catch the post. Will write to-morrow.

"Your loving daughter,
"MAGGIE."

P.S.—Nick says there *is* a reason for her wire. She will tell me after tea. She is very queer and jumpy."

"The voice of the dead," said Poirot, quietly. "And it tells us—nothing."

"The box by the gate," I remarked idly. "That's where Croft said he posted the will."

"Said so—yes. I wonder. How I wonder !"

"There is nothing else of interest among your letters ? "

"Nothing. Hastings, I am very unhappy. I am in the dark. Still in the dark. I comprehend nothing."

At that moment the telephone rang. Poirot went to it.

Immediately I saw a change come over his face. His manner was very restrained, nevertheless he could not disguise from my eyes his intense excitement.

His own contributions to the conversation were entirely non-committal so that I could not gather what it was all about.

Presently, however, with a *" Tres bien. Je vous remercie,"* he put back the receiver and came back to where I was sitting. His eyes were sparkling with excitement.

" Mon ami," he said. *" What did I tell you ?* Things have begun to happen."

" What was it ? "

" That was M. Charles Vyse on the telephone. He informs me that this morning, through the post, he has received a will signed by his cousin, Miss Buckley, and dated the 25th of February last."

" What ? *The* will ? "

" Évidément."

" It has turned up ? "

" Just at the right moment, *n'est ce pas ?* "

" Do you think he is speaking the truth ? "

" Or do I think he has had the will all along ? Is that what you would say ? Well, it is all a little curious. But one thing is certain; I told you that, if Mademoiselle Nick were supposed to be dead, we should have developments—and sure enough here they are ! "

" Extraordinary," I said. " You were right. I

suppose this is the will making Frederica Rice
residuary legatee ? "

" M. Vyse said nothing about the contents of the
will. He was far too correct. But there seems very
little reason to doubt that this is the same will. It
is witnessed, he tells me, by Ellen Wilson and her
husband."

" So we are back at the old problem," I said.
" Frederica Rice."

" The enigma ! "

" Frederica Rice," I murmured, inconsequently.
" It's a pretty name."

" Prettier than what her friends call her. Freddie "
—he made a face—" *ce n'est pas jolie*—for a young
lady."

" There aren't many abbreviations of Frederica,"
I said. " It's not like Margaret where you can
have half a dozen—Maggie, Margot, Madge,
Peggie——"

" True. Well, Hastings, are you happier now ?
That things have begun to happen ? "

" Yes, of course. Tell me—did you expect *this* to
happen ? "

" No—not exactly. I had formulated nothing very
precise to myself. All I had said was that given a
certain result, the causes of that result must make
themselves evident."

" Yes," I said, respectfully.

" What was it that I was going to say just as that
telephone rang ? " mused Poirot. " Oh, yes, that
letter from Mademoiselle Maggie. I wanted to look
at it once again. I have an idea in the back of my

mind that something in it struck me as rather curious."

I picked it up from where I had tossed it, and handed it to him.

He read it over to himself. I moved about the room, looking out of the window and observing the yachts racing on the bay.

Suddenly an exclamation startled me. I turned round. Poirot was holding his head in his hands and rocking himself to and fro, apparently in an agony of woe.

" Oh ! " he groaned. " But I have been blind—blind."

" What's the matter ? "

" Complex, I have said ? Complicated ? *Mais non*. Of a simplicity extreme—extreme. And miserable one that I am, I saw nothing—nothing."

" Good gracious, Poirot, what is this light that has suddenly burst upon you ? "

" Wait—wait—do not speak ? I must arrange my ideas. Rearrange them in the light of this discovery so stupendous."

Seizing his list of questions, he ran over them silently, his lips moving busily. Once or twice he nodded his head emphatically.

Then he laid them down and leaning back in his chair he shut his eyes. I thought at last that he had gone to sleep.

Suddenly he sighed and opened his eyes.

" But, yes ! " he said. " It all fits in ! All the things that have puzzled me. All the things that have seemed to me a little unnatural. They all have their place."

" You mean—you know everything ? "

" Nearly everything. All that matters. In some respects I have been right in my deductions. In other ways ludicrously far from the truth. But now it is all clear. I shall send to-day a telegram asking two questions—but the answers to them I know already —I know *here* ! " He tapped his forehead.

" And when you receive the answers ? " I asked, curiously.

He sprang to his feet.

" My friend, do you remember that Mademoiselle Nick said she wanted to stage a play at End House ? To-night, we stage such a play in End House. But it will be a play produced by Hercule Poirot. Mademoiselle Nick will have a part to play in it." He grinned suddenly. " You comprehend, Hastings, *there will be a ghost in this play*. Yes, a ghost. End House has never seen a ghost. It will have one to-night. No "—as I tried to ask a question—" I will say no more. To-night, Hastings, we will produce our comedy—and reveal the truth. But now, there is much to do—much to do."

He hurried from the room.

CHAPTER XIX

POIROT PRODUCES A PLAY

It was a curious gathering that met that night at End House.

I had hardly seen Poirot all day. He had been out for dinner but had left me a message that I was to be at End House at nine o'clock. Evening dress, he had added, was not necessary.

The whole thing was like a rather ridiculous dream.

On arrival I was ushered into the dining-room, and when I looked round I realised that every person on Poirot's list from A. to I. (J. was necessarily excluded, being in the Mrs. Harris-like position of " there ain't no sich person ") was present.

Even Mrs. Croft was there in a kind of invalid chair. She smiled and nodded at me.

" This is a surprise, isn't it ? " she said, cheerfully. " It makes a change for me, I must say. I think I shall try and get out now and again. All M. Poirot's idea. Come and sit by me, Captain Hastings. Somehow I feel this is rather a gruesome business—but Mr. Vyse made a point of it."

" Mr. Vyse ? " I said, rather surprised.

Charles Vyse was standing by the mantelpiece. Poirot was beside him talking earnestly to him in an undertone.

I looked round the room. Yes, they were all there. After showing me in (I had been a minute or two late) Ellen had taken her place on a chair just beside the door. On another chair, sitting painfully straight and breathing hard, was her husband. The child, Alfred, squirmed uneasily between his father and mother.

The rest sat round the dining-table. Frederica in her black dress, Lazarus beside her, George Challenger and Croft on the other side of the table. I sat a little away from it near Mrs. Croft. And now Charles Vyse, with a final nod of the head, took his place at the head of the table, and Poirot slipped unobtrusively into a seat next to Lazarus.

Clearly the producer, as Poirot had styled himself, did not propose to take a prominent part in the play. Charles Vyse was apparently in charge of the proceedings. I wondered what surprises Poirot had in store for him.

The young lawyer cleared his throat and stood up. He looked just the same as ever, impassive, formal and unemotional.

" This is rather an unconventional gathering we have here to-night," he said. " But the circumstances are very peculiar. I refer, of course, to the circumstances surrounding the death of my cousin, Miss Buckley. There will have, of course, to be an autopsy—there seems to be no doubt that she met her death by poison, and that that poison was administered with the intent to kill. This is police business and I need not go into it. The police would doubtless prefer me not to do so.

" In an ordinary case, the will of a deceased person is read after the funeral, but in deference to M. Poirot's especial wish, I am proposing to read it before the funeral takes place. In fact, I am proposing to read it here and now. That is why everyone has been asked to come here. As I said just now, the circumstances are unusual and justify a departure from precedent.

" The will itself came into my possession in a somewhat unusual manner. Although dated last February, it only reached me by post this morning. However, it is undoubtedly in the handwriting of my cousin—I have no doubt on that point, and though a most informal document, it is properly attested."

He paused and cleared his throat once more.

Every eye was upon his face.

From a long envelope in his hand, he drew out an enclosure. It was, as we could see, an ordinary piece of End House notepaper with writing on it.

" It is quite short," said Vyse. He made a suitable pause, then began to read:

" *This is the last Will and Testament of Magdala Buckley. I direct that all my funeral expenses should be paid and I appoint my cousin Charles Vyse as my executor. I leave everything of which I die possessed to Mildred Croft in grateful recognition of the services rendered by her to my father, Philip Buckley, which services nothing can ever repay.*
" *Signed*—MAGDALA BUCKLEY,
" *Witnesses*—ELLEN WILSON.
" WILLIAM WILSON."

P

I was dumfounded! So I think was everyone else. Only Mrs. Croft nodded her head in quiet understanding.

"It's true," she said, quietly. "Not that I ever meant to let on about it. Philip Buckley was out in Australia, and if it hadn't been for me—well, I'm not going into that. A secret it's been and a secret it had better remain. She knew about it, though. Nick did, I mean. Her father must have told her. We came down here because we wanted to have a look at the place. I'd always been curious about this End House Philip Buckley talked of. And that dear girl knew all about it, and couldn't do enough for us. Wanted us to come and live with her, she did. But we wouldn't do that. And so she insisted on our having the lodge—and not a penny of rent would she take. We pretended to pay it, of course, so as not to cause talk, but she handed it back to us. And now—this! Well, if anyone says there is no gratitude in the world, I'll tell them they're wrong! This proves it."

There was still an amazed silence. Poirot looked at Vyse.

"Had you any idea of this?"

Vyse shook his head.

"I knew Philip Buckley had been in Australia. But I never heard any rumours of a scandal there."

He looked inquiringly at Mrs. Croft.

She shook her head.

"No, you won't get a word out of me. I never have said a word and I never shall. The secret goes to the grave with me."

Vyse said nothing. He sat quietly tapping the table with a pencil.

" I presume, M. Vyse "—Poirot leaned forward—" that as next of kin you could contest that will ? There is, I understand, a vast fortune at stake which was not the case when the will was made."

Vyse looked at him coldly.

" The will is perfectly valid. I should not dream of contesting my cousin's disposal of her property."

" You're an honest fellow," said Mrs. Croft, approvingly. " And I'll see you don't lose by it."

Charles shrank a little from this well-meant but slightly embarrassing remark.

" Well, Mother," said Mr. Croft, with an elation he could not quite keep out of his voice. " This *is* a surprise ! Nick didn't tell *me* what she was doing."

" The dear sweet girl," murmured Mrs. Croft, putting her handkerchief to her eyes. " I wish she could look down and see us now Perhaps she does—who knows ? "

" Perhaps," agreed Poirot.

Suddenly an idea seemed to strike him. He looked round.

" An idea ! We are all here seated round a table. Let us hold a *séance*."

" A *séance* ? " said Mrs. Croft, somewhat shocked. " But surely——"

" Yes, yes, it will be most interesting. Hastings, here, has pronounced mediumistic powers." (Why fix on *me*, I thought.) " To get through a message from the other world—the opportunity is unique !

I feel the conditions are propitious. You feel the same, Hastings."

" Yes," I said resolutely, playing up.

" Good. I knew it. Quick, the lights."

In another minute he had risen and switched them off. The whole thing had been rushed on the company before they had had the energy to protest had they wanted to do so. As a matter of fact they were, I think, still dazed with astonishment over the will.

The room was not quite dark. The curtains were drawn back and the window was open for it was a hot night, and through those windows came a faint light. After a minute or two, as we sat in silence, I began to be able to make out the faint outlines of the furniture. I wondered very much what I was supposed to do and cursed Poirot heartily for not having given me my instructions beforehand.

However, I closed my eyes and breathed in a rather stertorous manner.

Presently Poirot rose and tiptoed to my chair. Then returning to his own, he murmured.

" Yes, he is already in a trance. Soon—things will begin to happen."

There is something about sitting in the dark, waiting, that fills one with unbearable apprehension. I know that I myself was a prey to nerves and so, I was sure, was everyone else. And yet I had at least an idea of what was about to happen. I knew the one vital fact that no one else knew.

And yet, in spite of all that, my heart leapt into my mouth as I saw the dining-room door slowly opening.

It did so quite soundlessly (it must have been oiled) and the effect was horribly grisly. It swung slowly open and for a minute or two that was all. With its opening a cold blast of air seemed to enter the room. It was, I suppose, a common or garden draught owing to the open window, but it *felt* like the icy chill mentioned in all the ghost stories I have ever read.

And then we all saw it ! Framed in the doorway was a white shadowy figure. Nick Buckley . . .

She advanced slowly and noiselessly—with a kind of floating ethereal motion that certainly conveyed the impression of nothing human. . . .

I realised then what an actress the world had missed. Nick had wanted to play a part at End House. Now she was playing it, and I felt convinced that she was enjoying herself to the core. She did it perfectly.

She floated forward into the room—and the silence was broken.

There was a gasping cry from the invalid chair beside me. A kind of gurgle from Mr. Croft. A startled oath from Challenger. Charles Vyse drew back his chair, I think. Lazarus leaned forward. Frederica alone made no sound or movement.

And then a scream rent the room. Ellen sprang up from her chair.

" It's her ! " she shrieked. " She's come back. She's walking ! Them that's murdered always walks. It's her ! It's her ! "

And then, with a click the lights went on.

I saw Poirot standing by them, the smile of the

ringmaster on his face. Nick stood in the middle of the room in her white draperies.

It was Frederica who spoke first. She stretched out an unbelieving hand—touched her friend.

" Nick," she said. " You're—you're *real* ! "

It was almost a whisper.

Nick laughed. She advanced.

" Yes," she said. " I'm real enough. Thank you so much for what you did for my father, Mrs. Croft. But I'm afraid you won't be able to enjoy the benefit of that will just yet."

" Oh, my God," gasped Mrs. Croft. " Oh, my God." She twisted to and fro in her chair. " Take me away, Bert. Take me away. It was all a joke, my dear—all a joke, that's all it was. Honest."

" A queer sort of joke," said Nick.

The door had opened again and a man had entered so quietly that I had not heard him. To my surprise I saw that it was Japp. He exchanged a quick nod with Poirot as though satisfying him of something. Then his face suddenly lit up and he took a step forward towards the squirming figure in the invalid chair.

" Hello-ello-ello," he said. " What's this ? An old friend ! Milly Merton, I declare ! And at your old tricks again, my dear."

He turned round in an explanatory way to the company, disregarding Mrs. Croft's shrill protests.

" Cleverest forger we've ever had, Milly Merton. We knew there had been an accident to the car they made their last getaway in. But there ! Even an injury to the spine wouldn't keep Milly from her tricks. She's an artist, she is!"

" Was that will a forgery ? " said Vyse.

He spoke in tones of amazement.

" Of course it was a forgery," said Nick scornfully. " You don't think I'd make a silly will like that, do you ? I left you End House, Charles, and everything else to Frederica."

She crossed as she spoke and stood by her friend, and just at that moment *it happened!*

A spurt of flame from the window and the hiss of a bullet. Then another and the sound of a groan and a fall outside. . . .

And Frederica on her feet with a thin trickle of blood running down her arm. . . .

CHAPTER XX

J.

It was all so sudden that for a moment no one knew what had happened.

Then, with a violent exclamation, Poirot ran to the window. Challenger was with him.

A moment later they reappeared, carrying with them the limp body of a man. As they lowered him carefully into a big leather armchair and his face came into view, I uttered a cry.

"*The face—the face at the window. . . .*"

It was the man I had seen looking in on us the previous evening. I recognised him at once. I realised that when I had said he was hardly human I had exaggerated as Poirot had accused me of doing.

Yet there was something about this face that justified my impression. It was a lost face—the face of one removed from ordinary humanity.

White, weak, depraved—it seemed a mere mask—as though the spirit within had fled long ago.

Down the side of it there trickled a stream of blood.

Frederica came slowly forward till she stood by the chair.

Poirot intercepted her.

"You are hurt, Madame?"

She shook her head.

" The bullet grazed my shoulder—that is all."

She put him aside with a gentle hand and bent down.

The man's eyes opened and he saw her looking down at him.

" I've done for you this time, I hope," he said in a low vicious snarl, and then, his voice changing suddenly till it sounded like a child's, " Oh ! Freddie, I didn't mean it. I didn't mean it. You've always been so decent to me. . . ."

" It's all right——"

She knelt down beside him.

" I didn't mean——"

His head dropped. The sentence was never finished.

Frederica looked up at Poirot.

" Yes, Madame, he is dead," he said, gently.

She rose slowly from her knees and stood looking down at him. With one hand she touched his fore-head—pitifully, it seemed. Then she sighed and turned to the rest of us.

" He was my husband," she said, quietly.

" J.," I murmured.

Poirot caught my remark, and nodded a quick assent.

" Yes," he said softly. " Always I felt that there was a J. I said so from the beginning, did I not ? "

" He was my husband," said Frederica again. Her voice was terribly tired. She sank into a chair that Lazarus brought for her. " I might as well tell you everything—now."

" He was—completely debased. He was a drug fiend. He taught me to take drugs. I have been fighting the habit ever since I left him. I think—at last—I am nearly cured. But it has been—difficult. Oh! so horribly difficult. Nobody knows how difficult!

" I could never escape from him. He used to turn up and demand money—with threats. A kind of blackmail. If I did not give him money he would shoot himself. That was always his threat. Then he took to threatening to shoot *me*. He was not responsible. He was mad—crazy. . . .

" I suppose it was he who shot Maggie Buckley. He didn't mean to shoot her, of course. He must have thought it was me.

" I ought to have said, I suppose. But, after all, I wasn't *sure*. And those queer accidents Nick had —that made me feel that perhaps it wasn't him after all. It might have been someone quite different.

" And then—one day—I saw a bit of his handwriting on a torn piece of paper on M. Poirot's table. It was a part of a letter he had sent me. I knew then that M. Poirot was on the track.

" Since then I have felt that it was only a matter of time. . . .

" But I don't understand about the sweets. He wouldn't have wanted to poison *Nick*. And anyway, I don't see how he *could* have had anything to do with that. I've puzzled and puzzled."

She put both hands to her face, then took them away and said with a queer pathetic finality:

" That's all. . . ."

CHAPTER XXI

THE PERSON—K.

LAZARUS came quickly to her side.

" My dear," he said. " My dear."

Poirot went to the sideboard, poured out a glass of wine and brought it to her, standing over her while she drank it.

She handed the glass back to him and smiled.

" I'm all right now," she said. " What—what had we better do next ? "

She looked at Japp, but the Inspector shook his head. " I'm on a holiday, Mrs. Rice. Just obliging an old friend—that's all I'm doing. The St. Loo police are in charge of the case."

She looked at Poirot.

"And M. Poirot is in charge of the St. Loo police ? "

" Oh ! *quelle idée, Madame !* I am a mere humble adviser."

" M. Poirot," said Nick. " Can't we hush it up ? "

" You wish that, Mademoiselle ? "

" Yes. After all—I'm the person most concerned. And there will be no more attacks on me—now."

" No, that is true. There will be no more attacks on you now."

" You're thinking of Maggie. But, M. Poirot, nothing will bring Maggie back to life again ? If you make all this public, you'll only bring a terrible lot

235

of suffering and publicity on Frederica—and she hasn't deserved it."

" You say she has not deserved it ? "

" Of course she hasn't ! I told you right at the beginning that she had a brute of a husband. You've seen to-night—what he was. Well, he's dead. Let that be the end of things. Let the police go on looking for the man who shot Maggie. They just won't find him, that's all."

" So that is what you say, Mademoiselle ? *Hush it all up.*"

" Yes. Please. Oh ! *please*. Please, *dear* M. Poirot."

Poirot looked slowly round.

" What do you all say ? '

Each spoke in turn.

" I agree," I said, as Poirot looked at me.

" I, too," said Lazarus.

" Best thing to do," from Challenger.

" Let's forget everything that's passed in this room to-night." This very determinedly from Croft.

" You *would* say that ! " interpolated Japp.

" Don't be hard on me, dearie," his wife sniffed to Nick, who looked at her scornfully but made no reply.

" Ellen ? "

" Me and William won't say a word, sir. Least said, soonest mended."

" And you, M. Vyse ? "

" A thing like this can't be hushed up," said Charles Vyse. " The facts must be made known in the proper quarter."

" Charles ! " cried Nick.

" I'm sorry, dear. I look at it from the legal aspect."

Poirot gave a sudden laugh.

" So you are seven to one. The good Japp is neutral."

" I'm on holiday," said Japp, with a grin. " I don't count."

" Seven to one. Only M. Vyse holds out—on the side of law and order ! You know, M. Vyse, you are a man of character ! "

Vyse shrugged his shoulders.

" The position is quite clear. There is only one thing to do.

" Yes—you are an honest man. *Eh bien*—I, too, range myself on the side of the minority. *I, too, am for the truth.*"

" M. Poirot ! " cried Nick.

" Mademoiselle—you dragged me into the case. I came into it at your wish. You cannot silence me now."

He raised a threatening forefinger in a gesture that I knew well.

" Sit down—all of you, and I will tell you—the truth."

Silenced by his imperious attitude, we sat down meekly and turned attentive faces towards him.

" *Écoutez !* I have a list here—a list of persons connected with the crime. I numbered them with the letters of the alphabet including the letter J. J. stood for a person unknown—linked to the crime by one of the others. I did not know who J. was until to-night, *but I knew that there was such a person.* The events of to-night have proved that I was right.

" But yesterday, I suddenly realised that I had made a grave error. I had made an omission. I added another letter to my list. The letter K."

" Another person unknown ? " asked Vyse, with a slight sneer.

" Not exactly. I adopted J. as the symbol for a person unknown. Another person unknown would be merely another J. K. has a different significance. *It stands for a person who should have been included in the original list, but who was overlooked.*"

He bent over Frederica.

" Reassure yourself, Madame. *Your husband was not guilty of murder.* It was the person K. who shot Mademoiselle Maggie."

She stared.

" But who is K. ? "

Poirot nodded to Japp. He stepped forward and spoke in tones reminiscent of the days when he had given evidence in police courts.

" Acting on information received, I took up a position here early in the evening, having been introduced secretly into the house by M. Poirot. I was concealed behind the curtains in the drawing-room. When everyone was assembled in this room, a young lady entered the drawing-room and switched on the light. She made her way to the fireplace and opened a small recess in the panelling that appeared to be operated with a spring. She took from the recess a pistol. With this in her hand she left the room. I followed her and opening the door a crack I was able to observe her further movements. Coats and wraps had been left in the hall by the visitors on arrival.

The young lady carefully wiped the pistol with a
handkerchief and then placed it in the pocket of a
grey wrap, the property of Mrs. Rice——"

A cry burst from Nick.

" This is untrue—every word of it ! "

Poirot pointed a hand at her.

" *Voilà !* " he said. " *The person K.! It was
Mademoiselle Nick who shot her cousin, Maggie
Buckley.*"

" Are you mad ? " cried Nick. " Why should I kill
Maggie ? "

" In order to inherit the money left to her by
Michael Seton ! Her name too was Magdala Buckley
—and it was to her he was engaged—not you."

" You—you——"

She stood there trembling—unable to speak.
Poirot turned to Japp.

" You telephoned to the police ? "

" Yes, they are waiting in the hall now. They've
got the warrant."

" You're all mad ! " cried Nick, contemptuously.
She moved swiftly to Frederica's side. " Freddie,
give me your wrist-watch as—as a souvenir, will
you ? "

Slowly Frederica unclasped the jewelled watch
from her wrist and handed it to Nick.

" Thanks. And now—I suppose we must go
through with this perfectly ridiculous comedy."

" The comedy you planned and produced in End
House. Yes—but you should not have given the star
part to Hercule Poirot. That, Mademoiselle, was
your mistake—your very grave mistake."

CHAPTER XXII

THE END OF THE STORY

" You want me to explain ? "

Poirot looked round with a gratified smile and the air of mock humility I knew so well.

We had moved into the drawing-room and our numbers had lessened. The domestics had withdrawn tactfully, and the Crofts had been asked to accompany the police. Frederica, Lazarus, Challenger, Vyse and I remained.

" *Eh bien*—I confess it—I was fooled—fooled completely and absolutely. The little Nick, she had me where she wanted me, as your idiom so well expresses it Ah ! Madame, when you said that your friend was a clever little liar—how right you were ! How right !"

" Nick always told lies," said Frederica, composedly. " That's why I didn't really believe in these marvellous escapes of hers."

" And I—imbecile that I was—did ! "

" Didn't they really happen ? " I asked. I was, I admit, still hopelessly confused.

" They were invented—very cleverly—to give just the impression they did."

" What was that ? "

" They gave the impression that Mademoiselle Nick's life was in danger. But I will begin earlier than that. I will tell you the story as I have pieced

240

it out—not as it came to me imperfectly and in
flashes.

" At the beginning of the business then, we have
this girl, this Nick Buckley, young and beautiful,
unscrupulous, and passionately and fanatically
devoted to her home."

Charles Vyse nodded.

" I told you that."

" And you were right. Mademoiselle Nick loved
End House. But she had no money. The house was
mortgaged. She wanted money—she wanted it
feverishly—and she could not get it. She met this
young Seton at Le Touquet, he is attracted by her.
She knows that in all probability he is his uncle's heir
and that that uncle is worth millions. Good, her
star is in the ascendant, she thinks. But he is not
really seriously attracted. He thinks her good fun,
that is all. They meet at Scarborough, he takes her
up in his machine and then—the catastrophe occurs.
He meets Maggie and falls in love with her at first
sight.

" Mademoiselle Nick is dumfounded. Her cousin
Maggie whom she has never considered pretty ! But
to young Seton she is ' different.' The one girl in the
world for him. They become secretly engaged. Only
one person knows—has to know. That person is
Mademoiselle Nick. The poor Maggie—she is glad
that there is one person she can talk to. Doubtless
she reads to her cousin parts of her fiancé's letters.
So it is that Mademoiselle gets to hear of the will.
She pays no attention to it at the time. But it
remains in her mind.

Q

" Then comes the sudden and unexpected death of Sir Matthew Seton, and hard upon that the rumours of Michael Seton's being missing. And straight away an outrageous plan comes into our young lady's head. Seton does not know that her name is Magdala also. He only knows her as Nick. His will is clearly quite informal—a mere mention of a name. But in the eyes of the world Seton is her friend ! It is with *her* that his name has been coupled. If she were to claim to be engaged to him, no one would be surprised. *But to do that successfully Maggie must be out of the way.*

" Time is short. She arranges for Maggie to come and stay in a few days' time. Then she has her escapes from death. The picture whose cord she cuts through. The brake of the car that she tampers with. The boulder—that perhaps was natural and she merely invented the story of being underneath on the path.

" And then—she sees *my* name in the paper. (I told you, Hastings, everyone knew Hercule Poirot !) and she has the audacity to make *me* an accomplice ! The bullet through the hat that falls at my feet. Oh ! the pretty comedy. And I am taken in ! I believe in the peril that menaces her ! *Bon !* She has got a valuable witness on her side. I play into her hands by asking her to send for a friend.

" She seizes the chance and sends for Maggie to come a day earlier.

" How easy the crime is actually ! She leaves us at the dinner table and after hearing on the wireless that Seton's death is a fact, she starts to put her plan into action. She has plenty of time, then, to take Seton's letters to Maggie—look through them and select the few that will answer her purpose. These she places in her own room. Then, later, she and Maggie leave the fireworks and go back to the house. She tells her cousin to put on her shawl. Then stealing out after her, she shoots her. Quick, into the house, the pistol concealed in the secret panel (of whose existence she thinks nobody knows). Then upstairs. There she waits till voices are heard. The body is discovered. It is her cue.

" Down she rushes and out through the window.

" How well she played her part ! Magnificently ! Oh, yes, she staged a fine drama here. The maid, Ellen, said this was an evil house. I am inclined to agree with her. It was from the house that Mademoiselle Nick took her inspiration."

" But those poisoned sweets," said Frederica. " I still don't understand about that."

" It was all part of the same scheme. Do you not see that if Nick's life was attempted *after* Maggie was dead that absolutely settled the question that Maggie's death had been a mistake.

" When she thought the time was ripe she rang up Madame Rice and asked her to get her a box of chocolates."

" Then it *was* her voice ? "

" But, yes ! How often the simple explanation is the true one ! *N'est ce pas ?* She made her voice sound a little different—that was all. So that you might be in doubt when questioned. Then, when the box arrived—again how simple. She fills three of the chocolates with cocaine (she had cocaine with her, cleverly concealed), eats one of them and is ill—but not *too* ill. She knows very well how much cocaine to take and just what symptoms to exaggerate.

" And the card—*my* card ! *Ah ! Sapristi*—she has a nerve ! It *was* my card—the one I sent with the flowers. Simple, was it not ? Yes, but it had to be thought of. . . ."

There was a pause and then Frederica asked ɪ

" Why did she put the pistol in my coat ? "

" I thought you would ask that, Madame. It was bound to occur to you in time. Tell me—had it ever entered your head that Mademoiselle Nick no longer liked you ? Did you ever feel that she might—hate you ? "

" It's difficult to say," said Frederica, slowly. " We lived an insincere life. She *used* to be fond of me."

" Tell me, M. Lazarus—it is not a time for false modesty, you understand—was there ever anything between you and her ? "

" No." Lazarus shook his head. " I was attracted to her at one time. And then—I don't know why— I went off her."

" Ah ! " said Poirot, nodding his head sagely. " That was her tragedy. She attracted people—and then they ' went off her.' Instead of liking her better and better you fell in love with her friend. She began to hate Madame—Madame who had a rich friend behind her. Last winter when she made a will, she was fond of Madame. Later it was different.

" She remembered that will. She did not know that

Croft had suppressed it—that it had never reached its destination. Madame (or so the world would say) had got a motive for desiring her death. So it was to Madame she telephoned asking her to get the chocolates. To-night, the will would have been read, naming Madame her residuary legatee—and then the pistol would be found in her coat—*the pistol with which Maggie Buckley was shot.* If Madame found it, she might incriminate herself by trying to get rid of it."

"She must have hated me," murmured Frederica.

"Yes, Madame. You had what she had not—the knack of winning love, and *keeping* it."

"I'm rather dense," said Challenger, "but I haven't quite fathomed the will business yet?"

"No? That's a different business altogether—a very simple one. The Crofts are lying low down here. Mademoiselle Nick has to have an operation. She has made no will. The Crofts see a chance. They persuade her to make one and take charge of it for the post. Then, if anything happens to her—if she dies—they produce a cleverly forged will—leaving the money to Mrs. Croft with a reference to Australia and Philip Buckley whom they know once visited the country.

"But Mademoiselle Nick has her appendix removed quite satisfactorily so the forged will is no good. For the moment, that is. Then the attempts on her life begin. The Crofts are hopeful once more. Finally, I announce her death. The chance is too good to be missed. The forged will is immediately posted to M. Vyse. Of course, to begin with, they

naturally thought her much richer than she is. They
knew nothing about the mortgage."

"What I really want to know, M. Poirot," said
Lazarus, " is how you actually got wise to all this.
When did you begin to suspect ? "

"Ah ! there I am ashamed. I was so long—so
long. There were things that worried me—yes.
Things that seemed not quite right. Discrepancies
between what Mademoiselle Nick told me and what
other people told me. Unfortunately, I always be-
lieved Mademoiselle Nick.

"And then, suddenly, I got a revelation. Mademoiselle Nick made one mistake. She was too clever.
When I urged her to send for a friend she promised
to do so—and suppressed the fact that she had
already sent for Mademoiselle Maggie. It seemed to
her less suspicious—*but it was a mistake.*

"For Maggie Buckley wrote a letter home immediately on arrival, and in it she used one innocent
phrase that puzzled me : ' *I don't see why Nick should
have telegraphed for me the way she did. Tuesday
would have done just as well.*' What did that mention
of Tuesday mean ? *It could only mean one thing.*
Maggie had been coming to stay on Tuesday anyway.
But in that case Mademoiselle Nick had lied—or had
at anyrate suppressed the truth.

"And for the first time I looked at her in a different
light. I criticised her statements. Instead of be-
lieving them, I said, ' Suppose this were not true.'
I remembered the discrepancies. ' How would it be
if every time it was Mademoiselle Nick who was
lying and not the other person ? '

" I said to myself. Let us be simple. What has *really* happened ?

" And I saw that what had really happened was that *Maggie Buckley* had been killed. Just that ! But who could want Maggie Buckley dead ?

" And then I thought of something else—a few foolish remarks that Hastings had made not five minutes before. He had said that there were plenty of abbreviations for Margaret—Maggie, Margot, etc. And it suddenly occurred to me to wonder what was Mademoiselle Maggie's real name ?

" Then, *tout d'un coup*, it came to me ! Supposing her name was *Magdala* ! It was a Buckley name, Mademoiselle Nick had told me so. Two Magdala Buckleys. Supposing . . .

" In my mind I ran over the letters of Michael Seton's that I had read. Yes—there was nothing impossible. There was a mention of Scarborough— but Maggie had been in Scarborough with Nick— her mother had told me so.

" And it explained one thing which had worried me. Why were there so *few* letters ? If a girl keeps her love-letters at all, she keeps *all* of them. Why these select few ? Was there any peculiarity about them ?

" And I remembered that there was no *name* mentioned in them. They all began differently— but they began with a term of endearment. Nowhere in them was there the name—*Nick*.

" And there was something else, something that I ought to have seen at once—that cried the truth aloud."

" What was that ? "

" Why—this. Mademoiselle Nick underwent an operation for appendicitis on February 27th last. There is a letter of Michael Seton's dated March 2nd, and no mention of anxiety, of illness or anything unusual. That ought to have shown me that the letters were written to a *different person altogether*.

" Then I went through a list of questions that I had made. And I answered them in the light of my new idea.

" In all but a few isolated questions the result was simple and convincing. And I answered, too, another question which I had asked myself earlier. *Why did Mademoiselle Nick buy a black dress ?* The answer was that she and her cousin had to be dressed alike, with the scarlet shawl as an additional touch. That was the true and convincing answer, *not* the other. A girl would not buy mourning before she knew her lover was dead. She would be unreal—unnatural.

" And so I, in turn, staged my little drama. And the thing I hoped for happened ! Nick Buckley had been very vehement about the question of a secret panel. She had declared there was no such thing. But if there were—and I did not see why Ellen should have invented it—*Nick must know of it*. Why was she so vehement ? Was it possible that she had hidden the pistol there ? With the secret intention of using it to throw suspicion on somebody later ?

" I let her see that appearances were very black against Madame. That was as she had planned. As I foresaw, she was unable to resist the crowning proof. Besides it was safer for herself. That secret panel might be found by Ellen and the pistol in it !

" We are all safely in here. She is waiting outside for her cue. It is absolutely safe, she thinks, to take the pistol from its hiding place and put it in Madame's coat. . . .

" And so—at the last—she failed. . . ."

Frederica shivered.

" All the same," she said. " I'm glad I gave her my watch."

" Yes, Madame."

She looked up at him quickly.

" You know that too ? "

" What about Ellen ? " I asked, breaking in. " Did she know or suspect anything ? "

" No. I asked her. She told me that she decided to stay in the house that night because in her own phrase she ' thought something was up.' Apparently Nick urged her to see the fireworks rather too decisively. She had fathomed Nick's dislike of Madame. She told me that ' she felt in her bones something was going to happen,' but she thought it was going to happen to Madame. She knew Miss Nick's temper, she said, and she was always a queer little girl."

" Yes," murmured Frederica. " Yes, let us think of her like that. A queer little girl. A queer little girl who couldn't help herself. . . . I shall—anyway."

Poirot took her hand and raised it gently to his lips.

Charles Vyse stirred uneasily.

" It's going to be a very unpleasant business," he

said, quietly. "I must see about some kind of defence for her, I suppose."

"There will be no need, I think," said Poirot, gently. "Not if I am correct in my assumptions."

He turned suddenly on Challenger.

"That's where you put the stuff, isn't it ? " he said. "In those wrist-watches."

"I—I——" The sailor stammered—at a loss.

"Do not try and deceive me—with your hearty good-fellow manner. It has deceived Hastings—but it does not deceive *me*. You make a good thing out of it, do you not—the traffic in drugs—you and your uncle in Harley Street."

"M. Poirot."

Challenger rose to his feet.

My little friend blinked up at him placidly.

"You are the useful ' boy friend.' Deny it, if you like. But I advise you, if you do not want the facts put in the hands of the police—to go."

And to my utter amazement, Challenger did go. He went from the room like a flash. I stared after him open-mouthed

Poirot laughed.

"I told you so, *mon ami*. Your instincts are always wrong. *C'est épatant !* "

"Cocaine was in the wrist-watch——" I began.

"Yes, yes. That is how Mademoiselle Nick had it with her so conveniently at the nursing home. And having finished her supply in the chocolate box she asked Madame just now for hers *which was full*."

"You mean she can't do without it ? "

"*Non, non*. Mademoiselle Nick is not an addict.

Sometimes—for fun—that is all. But to-night she needed it for a different purpose. It will be a full dose this time."

" You mean——? " I gasped.

" It is the best way. Better than the hangman's rope. But pst! we must not say so before M. Vyse who is all for law and order. Officially I know nothing. The contents of the wrist-watch—it is the merest guess on my part."

" Your guesses are always right, M. Poirot," said Frederica.

" I must be going," said Charles Vyse, cold disapproval in his attitude as he left the room.

Poirot looked from Frederica to Lazarus.

" You are going to get married—eh ? "

" As soon as we can."

" And indeed, M. Poirot," said Frederica. " I am not the drug-taker you think. I have cut myself down to a tiny dose. I think now—with happiness in front of me—I shall not need a wrist-watch any more."

" I hope you will have happiness, Madame," said Poirot, gently. " You have suffered a great deal. And in spite of everything you have suffered, you have still the quality of mercy in your heart. . . ."

" I will look after her," said Lazarus. " My business is in a bad way, but I believe I shall pull through. And if I don't—well, Frederica does not mind being poor—with me."

She shook her head, smiling.

" It is late," said Poirot, looking at the clock. We all rose.

"We have spent a strange night in this strange house," Poirot went on. "It is, I think, as Ellen says, an evil house. . . ."

He looked up at the picture of old Sir Nicholas. Then, with a sudden gesture, he drew Lazarus aside.

"I ask your pardon, but, of all my questions, there is one still unanswered. Tell me, why did you offer fifty pounds for that picture? It would give me much pleasure to know—so as, you comprehend, to leave nothing unanswered."

Lazarus looked at him with an impassive face for a minute or two. Then he smiled.

"You see, M. Poirot," he said. "I am a dealer."

"Exactly."

"That picture is not worth a penny more than twenty pounds. I knew that if I offered Nick fifty, she would immediately suspect it was worth more and would get it valued elsewhere. Then she would find that I had offered her far more than it was worth. The next time I offered to buy a picture she would not have got it valued."

"Yes, and then ? "

"The picture on the far wall is worth at least five thousand pounds," said Lazarus drily.

"Ah ! " Poirot drew a long breath.

"Now I know everything," he said, happily.